SARASWATI'S WAY

SARASWATI'S WAY

MONIKA SCHRÖDER

Frances Foster Books

Farrar Straus Giroux | New York

Ganesh or Ganesha are alternate ways of spelling the name of the elephant-headed god. Usage varies in different parts of India depending on the transliteration from Sanskrit and on local custom.

Copyright © 2010 by Monika Schröder
All rights reserved
Distributed in Canada by D&M Publishers, Inc.
Printed in October 2010 in the United States of America
by RR Donnelley & Sons Company, Harrisonburg, Virginia
Designed by Natalie Zanecchia
First edition, 2010
10 9 8 7 6 5 4 3 2 1

www.fsgkidsbooks.com

Library of Congress Cataloging-in-Publication Data
Schröder, Monika, 1965–
     Saraswati's way / Monika Schröder.— 1st ed.
        p. cm.
     Summary: Leaving his village in rural India to find a better education, mathematically gifted, twelve-year-old Akash arrives at the New Delhi train station, where he relies on Saraswati, the Hindu goddess of knowledge, to guide him as he negotiates life on the street, resists the temptations of easy money, and learns whom he can trust.
     ISBN: 978-0-374-36411-3 (alk. paper)
     [1. Education—Fiction. 2. Mathematics—Fiction. 3. Hindu goddesses—Fiction. 4. New Delhi (India)—Fiction. 5. India—Fiction.] I. Title.

PZ7.S37955Sar 2010
[Fic]—dc22

                                                              2009037286

For Asha Sablok

SARASWATI'S WAY

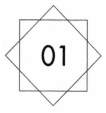

01

A light breeze blew plumes of sand across the empty schoolyard. On the other side of a low wall the flat desert stretched out against the horizon. Over the course of the morning, the dark rectangle this side of the wall would shrink, and by recess would provide just enough shade for children like Akash who didn't care to play cricket or run after a ball. From his seat by the open window Akash scanned the sky for signs of a rainstorm, for the swollen monsoon clouds that usually built up this time of year before they exploded with thunder and lightning to unleash sheets of rain. But the breeze only died, and Akash resigned himself to yet another day of relentless heat.

Mr. Sudhir was still performing the multiplication drill in front of the class. He pointed to a row of equations, leaving a white dot with his chalky index finger where he touched the blackboard. The students called the answers out in a loud chorus: 45, 54, 63. When would they see the pattern? It was so easy, once you saw the pattern in the numbers. Akash cited them backward in his mind, 81, 72, 63, 54, then added the multiplication products in his head, starting from the lowest. He knew the sequence and the total sum by heart. Numbers lined up in his head easily, arranged themselves into patterns, and moved in formations. Each math problem was like a hurdle he enjoyed jumping over with ease.

It was already too hot in the classroom. The blades of the old ceiling fan rotated slowly, cutting through the stale air more than moving it. Dark patches of sweat grew on the backs of the boys in front of him. The blue walls were covered with a patina of dirt, and a dark aura of smudge spread around the switches near the door. A faded black-and-white profile of Gandhi hung askew on the wall opposite the window. The old man looked serenely toward the lower left corner of the picture, his thin-rimmed, round glasses too low on his nose. Akash knew about

Gandhi—his birthday was a national holiday and the class had to memorize poems and songs in his honor. Gandhi had preached ahimsa, nonviolence, and had worn white, the color of truth. Gandhi had starved himself to show the British that his willpower was stronger than their weapons. Mr. Sudhir had explained to the class that Gandhi had also told Indians to stop wanting, that wanting only brought trouble. The other students had nodded, but Akash knew they all wanted something. Wanting was just another kind of hunger, burning until satisfied. Akash's family would soon not have enough to eat, because the rains hadn't come. But their hunger would not change anything. He focused on the dusty poster beside the door. Saraswati, the goddess of wisdom and knowledge, wore a white sari and played her stringed instrument, the veena. Like all Hindu gods she rode on a *vahana*, a creature that allowed her to travel the heavens. Saraswati's vehicle was a white swan, a sign of her wisdom and humility, according to Mr. Sudhir. Next to her feet waited a peacock. Akash locked his eyes onto Saraswati's pale face and made his daily wish to learn more math.

Since last January Mr. Sudhir had met with him twice a week before school to work on more difficult equations. His father had reminded Akash many times how lucky he was that the teacher took extra time to teach him math without asking for money. But this morning Mr. Sudhir had patted the old textbook in front of him after they had finished the last page. "This is all the math I know. I only finished tenth standard. I won't be able to help you any more." Akash had been worried that this moment would come. "Thank you for teaching me what you know," Akash had said after a short pause.

"If you do well in this year's final exams you might win a scholarship," the teacher had said.

"What is a scholarship?"

"A rich person or foundation gives money to the best students from poor families, to help them go to a good school so they can continue on to college."

"They have these scholarships for kids after seventh standard?"

"Yes. I wish I could find you a tutor to help you study."

"But I did well on my own last time."

"You were the sixth best last year in our district. Only the best student in the state wins the scholarship."

"How many students take the exam in the state?"

"Over one thousand."

Akash knew enough about probability to calculate his chances. In order to finish first he would need money to pay a tutor who could teach him what he needed to know. But his family didn't have any money.

"7 times 4," the teacher boomed now, shaking Akash out of the memory of this morning's conversation. The fan rotated two times. When no hand went up, the teacher pointed at a boy in the front row.

"Subash, what's the answer?"

"T-t-twenty-one," Subash stammered. The teacher shook his head.

"Akash!"

"28," Akash said. Subash turned around, and his angry glance hit Akash like the whip of a branch. Akash averted his eyes quickly and looked at Ravi, who sat next to him.

"Don't worry about him," Ravi whispered. "Just tell me the answer to the third one." Akash nodded, and when the teacher pointed to 9×7 Ravi raised his hand and answered, "63."

After school Ravi and Akash walked together back to their village. The path led straight along a turmeric field, separated from a dried-up irrigation canal by a long row of trees. The pollarded trees had shed their leaves in the intense heat. Their bare branches ended in thick knobs held upward like the fists of angry men. The drought had left the soil cracked, and the spice plants looked starved. Sometimes a short trickle of rain speckled the ground enough to give off the promising smell of wet mud. But after this cruel teaser the sky didn't open for a roaring downpour, gave no relief from the sticky heat that hung unchanged, like a punishment with no end in sight.

"How do you do it?" Ravi asked. "The answers just spill out of you."

"They're just in my head," Akash answered, kicking a pebble off the dirt path.

"They stick to you like flies on a cow," Ravi said. "Why are the numbers in your head and not in mine?"

"I don't know." Akash shrugged. He didn't like it when Ravi mentioned his gift for numbers. "But you can run faster than I can."

"Whoever gets to old Poonam's house second has to do the other one's homework," Ravi said. His eyes sparkled with the anticipated victory.

"All right." Akash knew he would lose this competition, but wanted to humor his friend.

"But you have to try!" Ravi called.

"I will," Akash said. "My legs just don't work as fast as my brain."

They crouched behind the line Ravi had quickly drawn in the dirt. "Go!" Ravi called, and disappeared instantly in a cloud of dust. Akash followed. There were eighteen trees between the school and the village. It took eleven steps to get from one tree to the next. That made 191 steps each way. If he knew the exact distance he could calculate Ravi's speed per kilometer. But Akash wouldn't suggest measuring it, for fear this would spoil the running fun for Ravi. Soon he heard Ravi's cry of victory. "First!" When Akash reached old Poonam's hut Ravi greeted him, laughing. "I thought you'd never get here!"

"Come on! I wasn't that slow!" said Akash, bending forward to catch his breath.

"Not fast enough for me to do your homework!" Ravi said, with a tone of triumph.

"No problem!" Akash said. "I'll do it!"

"Look, there is your uncle!" Ravi pointed in the direction of the banyan tree in the center of the village square, where three men sat on their charpoys, playing cards.

Akash quickly crossed the square without looking

up. He knew that his uncle would be losing money his family urgently needed. Akash waved goodbye and hurried toward his family's home at the western edge of the village. The narrow lane was empty and quiet at this time of day except for a few cows that stood motionless, blocking his path. The animals stared into the distance and showed no reaction to Akash's presence as he flattened himself against the wall to squeeze past one cow's bony shoulders.

Aunt Kamla was sweeping the hard mud in front of the hut with a twig broom, supporting her protruding pregnant belly with her free hand. Akash's little cousin Amit was playing in the shade and threw a handful of dirt in Akash's direction as he passed. Two tiny front teeth blinked in his broad smile.

Inside their two-room hut, his grandmother knelt in front of the family shrine. Dadima was dusting the painted clay statue of Ganesha, the elephant-headed god. Ganesha was worshipped as the remover of obstacles. With a dotted turban on his large head, he sat perched and smiling on a small mouse. Without taking notice of Akash, Dadima wiped the elephant's ears before she placed him next to the figure of Lakshmi, the goddess of prosperity. Saraswati was not present in Akash's family's shrine. But Mr. Sudhir had given Akash a small picture of Saraswati last February, when they celebrated Vasant Panchami, the goddess's birthday, in school. Akash had carried it in his notebook ever since. While Dadima still had her back turned to him, he opened the notebook and focused on the picture of the goddess. Akash put his hands together in front of his chest, whispering a short prayer to Saraswati, asking her to help him continue his education.

"Haven't you put your nose into books long enough at school?" Dadima got up and looked down at him disapprovingly. Folds of loose skin quivered on his grandmother's neck. "What are you dawdling in here for?" Akash quickly closed the notebook and put his schoolbag under the charpoy. "Get out and take your father his lunch. He's probably waiting for it already."

Akash hurried outside, where his cousin Anu was preparing for her daily walk to fetch water.

"You look like a bird that fell out of his nest," Anu said as she placed two small empty water vessels into a larger one and hoisted them on her hip. "What happened?"

"I need money for another teacher," Akash said, and picked up the two tiffin boxes with food that Dadima had placed for Bapu near the fire hole.

"What do you need another teacher for? Aren't you going to Mr. Sudhir's class?"

"Yes, but I need to find a tutor who knows more math so I can pass the exam as the best in the state."

"The best in the state?" Anu laughed. "What difference does it make? This is your last year of school anyway." It was easy for Anu to say. She had never gone to school. She couldn't read or write and the only numbers she knew were the ones she needed to count the goats. "I wish *I* had extra money," she continued. "Then I could buy new bangles at the Ganesha Chaturthi fair next week. But even if I had any money, it would need to go to my dowry so I'll find a good husband." Anu pulled the end of her sari over her face and turned toward the gate. Akash still hadn't gotten used to the sudden change in Anu since her thirteenth birthday last month. She was just a year older than him, but Anu was now obsessed with getting married. Akash remembered the visits from suitable boys' families just a year ago, when Aunt Kamla and Uncle Jagdish had been looking for a groom for Anu's older sister, his cousin

Asha. The boys' parents had looked at Asha the way Bapu inspected an ox he wanted to buy. He didn't understand how Anu could be excited about this prospect. Just like her older sister, Anu had no say in the matter and wouldn't even see her future husband before the ceremony. After the wedding she would need to move in with her husband's family and serve her new mother-in-law, just as her mother had to serve Dadima. Even so, girls seemed to live for their marriage day. He wouldn't say any more and followed her quickly through the gate before Dadima could remind him once again to take Bapu his food.

⌊…⌉

Bapu had tied a sheet between two *khejri* trees. Akash sat down with his father in the dark rectangle of the cloth's shade to have lunch. While he watched Bapu finish his food, Akash told him about his conversation with Mr. Sudhir in the morning.

"If we had any extra money we would need to give it to Kumar-ji," Bapu said as he wiped the tiffin box with the last piece of his chapati. "We owe him so much now that he is threatening to take away the land."

"But if he took the land we could never pay him back," Akash said.

"That's true. But he won't care." Bapu belched. "No, you will have to do well on your exam without any tutor. I'm sure you can pass it!"

"It's not about passing, Bapu. It's about scoring at the very top and winning the scholarship so I can go to a better school!" The words came out more forcefully than Akash had intended. Bapu turned to him and Akash saw a familiar sadness darkening his eyes. "Son, you are just as willful as your mother. She always wanted to change things for the better. She argued even with your Dadima." Bapu shook his head slowly. "Nothing changes because of our doing. It's all in the hands of the gods."

Akash wished he hadn't caused that sadness in Bapu. His mother had died giving birth to a sister when Akash was five years old. The baby had lived only three days. Akash often tried to force his memory to bring back his mother's face or what it had felt like when she touched him, but his attempts remained futile, like blowing the embers of a cold fire.

"What about Uncle Jagdish? If he worked we'd have more money." Akash had seen his uncle mix poppy husks with water and hastily drink the *bhukki* before he rested on his charpoy, his eyes mellow and soft from the opium.

"Your uncle is sick. All his thoughts are on the cards and the money he wins for the *bhukki*. He can't work!" Bapu frowned at him. Akash knew that asking Bapu why he didn't complain when Dadima gave money to Uncle Jagdish for playing cards or buying the poppy husk was like asking why Bapu didn't turn the desert sand into gold. Bapu was the younger of the brothers, and Dadima defended her older son as fiercely as a sow her litter. But the familiar anger grew in Akash, and for a moment he wished he were two years old instead of twelve and could throw himself flat on his stomach, pounding his fists on the ground and screaming how he wanted it to be different.

"Look!" Bapu pointed toward an acacia tree on the edge of the field, where a soft rustle drew their attention. A large tortoise slowly appeared from under the branches. The yellow-black star-shaped patterns on its shell blended perfectly with the colors of the desert shrubs.

"You don't see these very often anymore," Bapu said. "People now catch and sell them to other countries."

"What do they do with them in other countries?"

"In America people put tortoises in a cage to look at them."

"How do you know about this?"

Bapu stretched out in the shade. "Oh, I once saw a man selling two of them to the dentist at the Ganesha Chaturthi fair."

"How much money do they pay for a tortoise?"

"I don't know, but I don't think the gods made these tortoises to be sold to people in America," Bapu said. "I think they belong here."

Bapu closed his eyes and almost immediately began to snore. The festival commemorating Ganesha's birthday was coming up soon. Akash watched the tortoise crawl back into the bush. He could easily bring it to the Ganesha Chaturthi fair in Moti Bagh. He imagined the creature in a cage, surrounded by noisy children, pointing their fingers and throwing leaves. It would be wrong, but now the idea hummed in Akash's head like a bee caught in a glass.

02

Aunt Kamla had placed candles on the floor and the family squatted beside the fire. Anu ladled dal onto the tin plates and handed them to the men. The women would eat after the men were finished. On a small wooden board that she held between her thighs, Dadima rolled a clump of dough into a disk, then placed it onto the flat pan that she heated over the fire. The disk puffed up like a ball and let out a sigh when Dadima pressed it down with her fingers. She swiftly turned it over, again flattening it against the pan. When the chapati was evenly browned she handed it to Uncle Jagdish. The next one would be for Bapu, and Akash would be served third.

"Kumar-ji was here today," Dadima said. "He wanted his money."

No one spoke. Bapu and Uncle Jagdish kept their heads over their plates, using the bread to scoop dal into their mouths.

"I had no money to give him," she said, making another puffed-up bread sigh on the hot pan. "We owe him rent for eight months already."

"It's not our fault that the monsoon was bad this year," Bapu finally said.

"Kumar-ji doesn't care what the monsoon was like. He said if we don't pay by the end of this month, we need to come work for him."

"We have no one to send to work in his quarry. Who would work our land?" Bapu said.

"Akash should go." Dadima's words made Akash's stomach shrink.

"Akash has to go to school," Bapu said, looking at Dadima.

"Why teach a bucket to sing? He doesn't need to go to school past seventh standard," Dadima said.

"The teacher said he has real talent," Bapu said.

"Talent for what? He needs to help us. Kumar-ji

is hovering over us like a hawk over a mouse," Dadima said.

"The teacher said that the student with the best final exam result in the state will go to middle school in the city. We won't have to pay any money," Bapu said.

"If he is in a city school Akash won't even be here to help in the afternoons." The throw of her sari covered Aunt Kamla's face, but her words shot through the fabric like a camel's spit. "After we pay our debt we need to have a good dowry for Anu."

"Yes, that's another reason we need Akash to work," Dadima said. The candle light flickered over her prunelike face.

Bapu had turned his attention back to his food. Akash looked at Bapu, hoping he would catch his father's eye, make him say something else. He wished his mother were there. She might be able to convince Dadima.

"If I go to a better school, later I can earn lots of money to share with you," Akash heard himself say.

"Your head is full of dreams, just like your father's and his father's before that." Dadima threw the last chapati on her own plate and took the pan off the fire. "Dreams are like air. They don't feed our stomachs." She sucked her cheeks in and a smacking sound escaped her lips. "You will do what I tell you to do! And that is that!" With a nod she signaled Anu to take the dishes. Bapu left without looking up.

03

The next morning Akash woke up with a jolt. He felt Bapu's hand tapping on his shoulder. "Akash, I'm feeling hot. Go and fetch me some water!" Akash sat up. In the faint light from the small window behind his charpoy, Bapu's face glistened with sweat. Akash hurried outside, where Anu was pouring water from a vessel into a pitcher. Aunt Kamla lit the fire and the smell of hot oil and fried bread filled the yard. Dadima never slept much and she made sure that the other women didn't sleep long either. "I think Bapu caught the fever," Akash told Anu as he held a cup for her to fill next. "If he caught the fever you can't go to school," Anu said. "Dadima will send you to the field."

Back inside, Akash squatted next to Bapu's charpoy. Bapu drank the water quickly and leaned back with a sigh of pain. "Don't worry. I'll get better soon," Bapu said. But his voice sounded weak. Akash did worry. The fever came every August, at the end of the wet season, and each year people in the village died from it. "Would you like some breakfast?" Akash asked helplessly. Bapu just shook his head. A shadow fell over them from behind and Dadima's bony fingers clamped Akash's shoulder. "You go to the field. I'll take care of your father," Dadima ordered, in her crow's voice. Against hope Akash asked, "What can we do?"

"Go to work. Pray for him," she said, her silhouette darkening the doorframe as she stepped back outside.

Akash's family's field was at the end of the irrigation canal, and after the months of drought only a residue of dried mud was left where the water used to flow. If it didn't rain soon, the *kharif* crop would be ruined. The plants had reached only half their usual height. As Akash weeded carefully through the rows he noticed many leaves parched or marred by brown patches. Now he was tired and sat down under the tree where he had shared lunch with Bapu the day before. The gray-brown sky just hung like a dirty blanket without texture, compressing the thick moist air.

Akash focused on a spot in the far distance. He liked to play this game with himself. After a while the spot would melt into an image—sometimes he would see a camel, other days a bus driving toward him from the desert. Mr. Sudhir had told them this was called a mirage, caused by Earth's round shape and light rays broken through the heat. Today a white dome formed. It reminded Akash of the old calendar with a photo of the Taj Mahal that hung on the wall behind the teacher's desk. "This famous tomb is a monument to love," Mr. Sudhir had said, followed by a long silence. Akash had wondered what Mr. Sudhir knew about love, but he didn't dare to ask. Bapu talked about love only with the pained look of loss on his face. The white dome flickered in the heat, hovering over what looked like a bed of water. One day he wished to see this famous monument. With a blink he wiped away the mirage. His thoughts returned to his plan to sell a tortoise at the Ganesha Chaturthi fair. Ganesha was, after all, the remover of obstacles. This might be an auspicious time. But would Ganesha grant two wishes—make Bapu healthy and help

Akash get the money for a tutor? Dadima had asked him to walk with her to the fairground. He could carry the animal in a sack and find the dentist while Dadima climbed up to the temple for her *puja*.

Akash stood up to see if the tortoise was still there. His steps startled a field mouse. He stopped to watch it scurry along a short way before it paused. For a moment the mouse seemed to look at him, then hurried in the direction of the acacia tree, where it disappeared into a hole. Akash bent down to take a closer look at the pile of stones under the bush. And there it was. The large shell of the tortoise lay perfectly still, half shaded by a rock. Akash picked up the tortoise and turned it over. The animal tried to hide its head and legs inside the shell. It must be a female, since it had the longer claws needed to excavate a nest for its eggs. Maybe a female turtle would bring more money. Akash put the tortoise back on the ground and it crawled as quickly as it could under the rock. He felt a pang of guilt, remembering that Bapu had told him it was not right to cage a tortoise. But a tortoise couldn't find food easily during the drought. In America friendly people would feed it every day. And hadn't the mouse, Ganesha's vehicle, his *vahana*, shown Akash the way?

04

Bapu's fever continued for another two days. Akash dreaded the hopeless fieldwork and spent more and more time under the tree, staring into the distance, imagining himself in a different school, playing with numbers in his head, or letting mirages appear. On Friday afternoon, just as he was wondering how many hours of tutoring he could buy for the money he would get for the tortoise, he saw Ravi approaching the field.

"You already missed three days of school," Ravi said. "Lucky you!"

"My father is sick, so my Dadima sent me to work in the field," Akash said. He couldn't tell Ravi about his plan. He wouldn't understand. Everything was different for Ravi. His father was a *gujjar*, a herder. They didn't depend on the monsoon as much as farmers. Ravi's family didn't have to take out a loan. Ravi could go to school until tenth standard, at least. And he didn't even like school. Akash tried to shake off the envy that surged inside him.

"Today a group of boys from a city school came to our class," Ravi said. "They brought us books."

"What kind of books?"

"Fat books, written in English," Ravi said. "I took this one for you."

"Thank you." Akash opened the cover. The book was a textbook for learning English. Mr. Sudhir had taught Akash some English, had explained how the alphabet translated into Hindi letters. Akash flipped through the pages and stopped at a page titled "Unit 8—At School." A drawing of neatly dressed and combed students sitting at proper desks in front of a teacher in a Western suit accompanied the lesson.

"You should have seen these boys. All dressed in white shirts with the name of the school embroidered on their shirt pockets. They lined up, pressing their backs against the wall, and stared at us like we were three-horned cows. And they wore leather shoes with white socks. In this heat!"

Akash kept quiet, turning the pages in the text-book. He couldn't tell Ravi how badly he wanted to be one of those boys.

⌊…⌉

In the evening Bapu's fever still hadn't broken. He lay on his charpoy in the corner of the yard, tossing and turning under a sheet. Akash dampened a cloth in the water bucket and dabbed his father's forehead. "Bapu?" Bapu mumbled words that Akash could not understand. Bapu's eyes bulged out of his face, and his cheeks had already sunken deeply, showing the contours of his skull.

"This used to be your mother's favorite time of day," Bapu said, his voice raspy. He lifted his index finger slightly to point toward the sky. "*Godhuli*, the time of dusk."

Akash looked up. The sky had turned wild shades of red and purple, as if the gods had thrown colored powders to play Holi. "We used to go to the river to watch the cows come home. The clouds of dust kicked up by their hooves would smudge the red horizon. Your mother's face glowed beautifully in the soft reddish twilight." Akash moved a cup close to Bapu's lips. "You need to drink. The fever dries you out." Bapu took a sip and turned to Akash. Bapu was calmer now.

He held his gaze steadily on Akash, his eyes suddenly clear.

"*Godhuli* is also the time of day when the soul needs to go home," Bapu said quietly. "Always remember your parents at *godhuli*."

"Bapu!" Akash shuddered at the mention of death.

"Don't worry, son. What you desire is on its way," Bapu whispered, and closed his eyes. Akash wanted to ask what that meant, but Bapu's breathing had calmed. He shouldn't wake his father. Akash got up and walked inside the hut. Adorned by flower garlands, surrounded by *ladoos* and coconuts, Ganesha sat, his elephant eyes gleaming with self-content. Akash brought the palms of his hands together in front of his chest and bowed toward Ganesha, whispering a short prayer. Tomorrow morning, before he set out to Moti Bagh, he would go and catch the tortoise. Then Ganesha could prove that he was the remover of obstacles.

05

The tortoise was still in the underbrush where he had first seen it when Akash went to get it. He lined a sack with dried grass before he placed the tortoise inside and now carried it carefully over his shoulder as he walked with Dadima toward Moti Bagh.

They could see the hill from a distance. A colorful band of people crawled like ants up toward the temple at the top. Akash was thirsty and he was glad to see an earthen water jug with two cups attached by a long string standing in front of a house at the entry to Moti Bagh. He filled one of the two cups with water for Dadima. She nodded and gulped the water hastily. He waited until she had had three cups before he poured one for himself. The water made him feel fresh again and he straightened his back before he offered his arm to lead Dadima across the village to the fairground. The narrow street was full, with people on foot and in rickshaws and jeeps. Groups of cows slowly trotted along the side. The loud honking of a jeep startled Dadima, but instead of stepping out of the way she turned around and screamed at the driver, "You should honor an old woman and not scare me like this!" The driver just laughed and honked his horn again while Akash pulled Dadima aside. "Be careful." The jeep was loaded with more people than it had seats for, and young men were holding on to the metal frame as the driver jerked forward. The closer Akash and Dadima came to the fairground, the denser the crowd grew. Traffic crawled very slowly and the pedestrians had to move in a careful weave around the different vehicles and cows blocking the road. Young women wore shiny new saris and *lehngas*. A red *tilak* burned on the forehead of each worshipper who had already climbed up to the temple for *puja*. Akash and Dadima reached a parking lot filled with jeeps, rickshaws, and camel carts. On one side a path led upward toward the temple, while the other side marked the entrance to the fairground. Dadima stopped near an empty chair in front of a tea stall. "This is where you will wait for me," Dadima ordered. "I'll climb up to the temple alone." As Akash had expected, he would have some time to himself while Dadima did *puja*. "Make sure you're here when I return. We have to be back before dark." Akash nodded.

The fairground was covered with long rows of stalls. Every vendor played a different tape or radio station, filling the air with a cacophony of sound. Some of them sold food or juice; others offered farming equipment. For a moment Akash's eye clung to a table with sabers and daggers of various sizes. But he had to make good use of his time. He scanned the row of vendors for the dentist. A group of people gathered in a circle at an intersection. He couldn't resist and squeezed himself through the crowd to see what they were looking at. A tall man with a huge mustache dressed in a bright red kurta over baggy white pants stood in the middle of the crowd. His oily black hair was parted in the middle and grew down to his shoulders. In front of him lay a dark blue woolen blanket partially covering what seemed like a child's body. On one end two skinny brown legs stuck out, but did not move. The man in the red kurta circled the blanket in slow strides, followed by a small brown monkey on a leash. A shiver crawled up Akash's back as the man's dark eyes focused on him. Stepping closer and stopping right in front of Akash, the man asked, "Will the boy live?" Akash looked at the still legs but they didn't twitch. He wanted to ask, "What did you do to him?" but the words were stuck in his throat. A man in the audience called out, "Show him to us!"

"I will," answered the man with the large mustache. "But first I want to see how much you bid." He let the monkey off the leash to collect money from the bystanders. "Yes!" the crowd replied. "All right!" The man with the mustache waved his hand in a dramatic motion. He bent down and lifted the blanket. A gasp echoed through the audience. Akash held his breath. A boy his age lay on the floor with a sword stuck in his throat. "Can you say something?" the man asked the boy.

"What do you want me to say?" the boy answered, and Akash exhaled, together with the other people in the audience. Suddenly he felt a tug on his pants. The monkey looked at Akash, showing him the palm of its hand. "I don't have any money," Akash said to the monkey. "Then get away from here and make way for people who can pay for what they see!" The man jumped forward and clapped his hands in front of Akash's face as if to shoo away a fly.

Akash quickly wiggled his way out of the circle, cradling the tortoise in his arms, and walked back toward the square where he had left Dadima. He calculated the sum the man with the mustache would collect in a day. He had seen several men hand ten-rupee notes to the monkey. Some gave five-rupee coins. If only twenty people gave ten rupees he would have two hundred rupees. He could probably do the show two or three times a day. That would be about four to six hundred rupees daily. How much would he pay the boy?

On the other side of the midway he now saw the dentist squatted beside a blanket. The dentist was a Sikh. He wore a turban but his was not made from the thin pink-and-white-striped material that Uncle Jagdish and Bapu tied around their heads for special occasions, but from dark red cotton. Sikh men wore their turbans to cover their hair, which they considered holy. The men in Akash's family wore turbans to show which village they came from. Under an umbrella the dentist had arranged a display on a blue blanket. Individual teeth of different sizes and lengths lay beside a small pair of tweezers, a chisel, and a spoonlike device with a long handle.

"Do you have a toothache?" the dentist asked.

"No." Akash couldn't take his eyes off the teeth. "Did you pull these?"

"Yes, these and many more," the dentist answered. "But if you don't need my services you should move on."

"I'd like to ask you something else," Akash began. "I've heard that you like to buy tortoises."

The dentist stood up and straightened his back. "Is that true?" Akash continued.

"That depends," the dentist said.

"I would like to sell you one." Akash lifted his bag and stepped closer. He opened the bag and held it toward the dentist. The dentist looked inside before he let his arm disappear in the bag. He pulled the tortoise out, but its head and legs hung limply out of its shell. "It's dead," he said, handing it back to Akash.

06

apu's charpoy was empty when they returned from the fair. Anu came running toward them, her face puffy from crying. "Your Bapu died," she called, throwing her arms around Akash. Dadima wailed like a wounded animal and ran inside the hut. Anu let go of Akash, dried her tears with the throw of her sari, and followed Dadima. Bapu's sheet lay on the ground beside the charpoy. They must have moved him from his bed to the ground to make sure he was in contact with the earth at the moment of death. Akash tried to remember his last conversation with Bapu. "What you desire is on its way," he had said, when they had looked at the purple-red evening sky. How could this be true now? Pain flooded

Akash like blood soaking a cloth. He had been angry at Bapu for not supporting his wish to get a tutor. And Bapu had told him that tortoises belonged in the desert. Had Yama, the god of death, taken Bapu to punish Akash?

Akash closed his eyes for a moment to see if this was just a bad dream, but when he opened them again Bapu's charpoy was still empty. He sat down, picked up the sheet, and pressed it against his face, inhaling the sour smell of Bapu's sweat. When he looked up Akash saw Uncle Jagdish entering the yard with the neighbors and Uncle Pakaj, who lived at the other end of the village. The news of Bapu's death must have traveled fast, since neighbors and relatives had already arrived to help prepare for the cremation. The men's kurtas were soiled with dark streaks. They had come back from building the pyre. Hindu customs demanded the cremation of the deceased before nightfall. Dusk could only be another hour away. They would burn Bapu's body soon.

Suddenly, Akash's head was pressed against the warm, damp rolls of flesh of a woman's body. "Akash! My poor boy!" Aunt Sula, his mother's sister, let go of him with a loud sob. Akash got up and she pulled him again toward her soft midriff. "Come!" she called, and led him inside the hut. When Akash's eyes had adjusted he saw his father's body lying on a pallet in the middle of the small room, covered with a white sheet. Uncle Jagdish, Dadima, and the other relatives stood with their backs against the walls, and Akash could feel everyone's gaze on him as he stepped closer to Bapu's dead body. Dadima pressed a garland of marigolds into Akash's hand, and he bent over Bapu's head to put the flowers around his neck. Akash shuddered at the touch of Bapu's stiff, bony shoulders. Pandit-ji, the village priest, stood near the foot of the pallet, hands folded above his paunch, mumbling a prayer through his unkempt beard. Akash tried not to look at Bapu's face, but his eyes kept moving back to Bapu's sunken cheeks, the dark hollows of his temples, and the bright orange *tilak* Pandit-ji had drawn on his forehead. On his signal Uncle Jagdish, together with Cousin Asha's husband and two other men, lifted the pallet with the body. The men would go to the cremation site while the women stayed behind, cleaning the house. Akash and Pandit-ji followed the small procession as they left the yard to carry Bapu to the river. From the rim of the pallet dangled the chain of marigolds swaying in the rhythm of the men's steps. Akash began to chant, *"Ram naam satya hai, satya se mugat hai." Only the name of God is truth and the truth paves the way for salvation.* They reached the riverbank, where the pallet was placed on a pile of logs. Pandit-ji circled the pyre, ladling ghee onto the woodpile from an earthen pot. As the only son of the deceased Akash was the first family member to perform the necessary rituals during the cremation. He finished pouring the ghee and handed the pot to Uncle Jagdish. Bapu's feet pointed southward to make it easy for his soul to escape in the direction of Yama's abode. When enough ghee was poured onto the pyre, Akash lit the fire. The wind was kind and blew the smoke away from the small crowd and over the thin rivulet that was left of the river. After the fire had burned for a long time, Pandit-ji called Akash to step closer to the pyre and handed him a long bamboo pole. Akash let it sink quickly onto Bapu's skull, which broke with a crack. Akash strained his eyes but could not see Bapu's soul leave the pyre. There were only the fluttering veils of the orange flames leaping from the glowing logs and then, as they died down, nothing.

With the other men Akash stepped into the thin stream for their purifying bath. He let the lukewarm water rinse over his upper body and tried not to think. But the water could not wash away the pain of life without Bapu. No one spoke when they walked away without looking back.

It was getting dark when they returned to the hut. Akash put on the white clothes Dadima pressed into his hands. The barber came and shaved Uncle Jagdish's head. Then he called Akash to sit down. Akash watched the tufts of his hair glide down to the ground. When Akash passed a plate with *ladoos* left from Ganesha's birthday, he forgot one of the many strict rules for mourners. No sweets were allowed. When Akash tried to put a *ladoo* into his mouth, Dadima slapped his hand and yelled, "Do you want your father to turn into a soulless ghost?" But it was Akash who felt like he had lost his soul.

07

When are we leaving?" Akash asked on the morning of the third day after Bapu's death. On this day custom demanded that the ashes of the deceased be collected and immersed in the river Ganga. A few years ago, after his grandfather had died, the family had taken a bus to Haridwar, a holy city at the Ganga. Akash remembered the long, bumpy ride in the bus through a cold night and their arrival in the early morning, the city covered in chilly fog. On their way to the riverbank Bapu had pointed out the black silhouette of the tall Shiva statue growing out of the dark orange morning sky. Akash had never seen a broader river and Bapu had shown him *hari-ki-pairi*, the place where a drop of nectar had fallen from the churning of the oceans when the world was created and the gods took their first steps on Earth. In spite of the cold, people were undressing to take a dip in the holy river near the auspicious site. Lord Vishnu's footprint was engraved on the steps and Akash had wondered how small the god's feet must have been. Near the bank of the river Dadima had hired a priest to perform the necessary rituals before she scattered the ashes in the fast-moving stream.

Now, Dadima just shook her head and said, "No, we won't go to Haridwar. We don't have money for the trip."

"But don't Bapu's ashes need to be put into the holy water for his soul to be released?"

"Pandit-ji will take you to the stream and you will put the ashes there. They will reach Mother Ganga from here." Dadima handed Akash an earthen urn, and a stern look on her face forbade any further questions. Akash wanted to protest but she had already turned toward the *puja* corner and was bowing down in front of the two statues for another prayer.

Later that morning Pandit-ji and Akash walked together back to the cremation ground. Uncle Jagdish followed. When they arrived at the riverbank Akash began to collect the ashes and remaining bones, carefully placing them in the urn. Uncle Jagdish found shade under a tree. The river had dried up almost completely, leaving a broad plane of cracked mud framing the narrow vein of shallow water. Akash followed Pandit-ji to the rim of the thin stream, where the priest spoke a prayer and let a few drops of holy Ganga water spill from his brass container onto Bapu's remains. Then Akash turned the urn upside down and let the ashes fall. For a moment they seemed to dance on the water's surface, reflecting the morning sun like the wings of tiny insects before they melted in the slow current.

It would have been better had they given Bapu's ashes directly into the Ganga, like Grandfather's. But the trip to Haridwar had taken place before Uncle Jagdish had started to take the *bhukki* and lose money with cards. Akash spoke another prayer, forcing himself not to show his anger, before they walked back to the riverbank. Uncle Jagdish opened his eyes and got up slowly as Akash and Pandit-ji came closer, steadying himself against the tree. His eyes were bloodshot from the *bhukki*. Akash glared at him. Why had Yama, the god of death, not taken Uncle Jagdish instead of Bapu?

08

In the afternoon Aunt Tanu, Bapu's older sister, arrived. Akash threw himself into her arms and buried his face in the folds of her sari. "Oh, Akash," she said, her eyes moist with tears. "I am sorry." Tanu was his favorite aunt but had married a man from a village that was two days' travel away. It was good to see Aunt Tanu. After she was greeted by all the other relatives she sat down with Akash in a corner of the yard.

"You will get through this, Akash," she said, stroking his bald head.

Akash swallowed and looked at his feet. Feelings and thoughts simmered in his head like the bubbles of air as hot water begins to boil. He couldn't hold them back anymore and in a gush of words and tears he told Aunt Tanu how he missed Bapu, how he felt responsible for Bapu's death, and how he wished he had never taken the tortoise. There was a silence when his sobbing ended.

"You think you have the power to direct Lord Yama?" Aunt Tanu asked. "It's not your fault that your Bapu died. He caught the fever. The tortoise didn't get enough air or food or maybe it was even ill before you took it. You can't blame yourself."

Aunt Tanu's words felt like a soothing wind.

"You will do well on this exam and then you can go to that other school," she continued, making the future sound so easy. Akash wanted to ask how the family would pay their debt, where the money for a tutor and Anu's dowry would come from. But he felt it was too selfish to admit more of his own worries.

"I remember when your father and I flew our kites and one got stuck in the neighbor's tree," Aunt Tanu now said, looking at him encouragingly, wanting him to let go of the despair. "He kept it there and told me that now the tree would grow more kites. And I believed him." She laughed. Akash could only smile, but he was thankful for her attempt to cheer him up.

"Look," she said, pulling a parcel out of her bag. "I brought you a present. Your Bapu gave it to me when I left the family after my wedding."

"It's a *dhabla*," Akash said, taking the thick woolen shawl from the paper.

"I thought you might need it more than I do. Our father gave it to him," Aunt Tanu said.

"Thank you," Akash said. It was too hot to wear a shawl but Akash wrapped it tightly across his shoulders and imagined it to be Bapu's arms.

09

On the thirteenth day after the cremation a service in the temple would celebrate the end of the family's most intense mourning period. It was still dark outside when Dadima and Akash left with the aunts and uncles for the temple. Akash carried the coconut, one of the offerings necessary for the *puja*. They each touched the temple's bell before taking off their shoes and climbing up the stairs to the sanctuary. The sound of the bell was still vibrating in Akash's empty stomach as they entered a dark room. Dadima handed the priest the camphor, and the old man brought the palms of his hands together in front of his bare chest and bowed three times toward the fire that burned on the stone altar. Then he lit the piece of camphor and slowly moved it over the flames. The fire's orange tongues licking against the darkness brought back the memory of the cremation. Agni, the god of fire, had released Bapu's soul. Now they thanked Agni for showing Bapu's soul the right way. Dadima nudged Akash to pass the coconut to the priest. The old man broke the round fruit with a loud whack of a machete, releasing the water into the fire. Agni appreciated the offering with a sizzle. The priest quartered the shell, left two pieces on the altar, and returned two pieces to Dadima, who would give them to the poor outside the temple. The priest began a prayer that ended in a chant. Dadima and the aunts and uncles accompanied him, and the small temple filled with their voices. Akash too joined in, letting the monotonous melody reverberate through his body. Now Bapu's soul was free. Akash hoped that by following all the rules he had helped Bapu to find peace in the afterlife. But he was left alone now, lonely in his own family. Aunt Tanu would have to take the bus back to her village. Bapu had said that what Akash desired was on its way. But even without help he would find a way for his longing to be fulfilled. Akash bent slightly forward to show the fire that he could withstand the pain of being lonely. The priest placed a dot of sandalwood paste on his forehead as if sealing Akash's resolution.

10

The next morning Akash woke up early. He
lay on his charpoy, thinking about his return
to school, and when voices came from the yard, he
hurried over to the window to see who was outside.
A tall man stood with his back to the hut, looking
down at Dadima, whose head only reached his chest.

"Kumar-ji, what brings you here so early in the
morning?" Dadima asked.

"I went by your field," he said. "You won't make
enough money from your crop to pay me back."

"I know," Dadima said. "I need more time."

"That's what you asked for last month, and the
month before. I can't wait any longer. Your debt grows
every month and you cannot even pay the interest."

"What do you want me to do? My son just died," Dadima said, rubbing her forearms with her bony hands.

"I am sorry for your loss, but I waited until the thirteenth day had passed. Now I need my payment," Kumar-ji said.

"Maybe the gods will send rain and we will sell some of our chickpeas," Dadima said, but her voice did not sound confident.

"Your crop is wilted. You need to send me someone to work to pay off your debt."

"Whom can I send?" Dadima asked, shrugging her shoulders. "My other son is sick."

"I can take your grandson. He is old enough to work for me."

"You will let me keep my land if I send Akash?" Dadima asked.

Kumar-ji bobbed his head. "Yes, but he needs to come with me right now."

⌊...⌉

Akash stormed out into the yard. "I can't go with him!" he yelled. "I have to go to school."

"I have told you before. You will do what I say!" Dadima looked at him, her face pulled into an angry frown.

"But why can't Uncle Jagdish work? Once I have finished school I will be able to find work that will pay better."

"I have had enough of your dreams. It won't hurt you to work. That will douse the fire inside you. You need to learn to take what is given." Dadima wagged her bony finger at him.

Akash ran inside and stuffed his textbook, a notebook, and Bapu's shawl into a canvas bag. "You won't change her," Anu said quietly as he passed her making the fire.

"And she won't change me," Akash called out, walking toward the jeep parked outside the gate.

11

Akash couldn't remember how long he had sat in the back of the jeep. At first he had counted the camel carts they passed in hopes that concentrating on numbers would calm his fear, but the worry about where Kumar-ji would take him wiped out all other thoughts. He knew they were going west because the rectangle of the windshield framed the sun's white ball. Akash wondered how Kumar-ji could sleep in the front seat. Every time the car jumped over a bump in the road, Kumar-ji's head bounced against the headrest, but his eyes remained closed. The jeep finally slowed down and turned onto a gravel road following the direction of an arrow-shaped sign that read KUMAR QUARRY—STONES OF

QUALITY. Uneven ruts scarred the road and Akash bounced on the backseat to the rhythm of the jarring jeep. Kumar-ji rubbed his eyes and let out a yawn as the driver finally stopped at the edge of a large field covered with mounds of coarse sand and gravel. Piles of stones graded by size lay as far as the eye could see. In the distance the field bordered a row of low brown hills, partly scraped open, exposing a lighter shaded surface. "Come!" Akash followed Kumar-ji, whose steps crunched ahead. They passed a group of women filling metal trays with gravel. When a tray was filled they slowly got up, straightened themselves, and helped one another to balance their loads on their heads. Then they trudged with their trays to a conveyer belt connected to a machine that rattled in a tight beat. Akash couldn't see what this machine did with the stones, since his view was partly obscured by large boulders that leaned against one another at awkward angles, as if a giant child had tried to build a tower with them. Boys in grimy undershirts sat on the ground, pounding stone blocks with hammers and chisels. The irregular rhythm of their pecking competed with the darker noises from the machines in the background. Next to them stood rectangular slabs of gray-brown stone stacked like huge, thick playing cards. Three girls in dusty saris, each balancing a metal tray with piles of cobblestones on her head, walked to the back of a truck, where a skinny man was waiting to add their heaps to the neat stack behind him.

"Here." Kumar-ji pointed to a rectangular block. "Sit down." A big man approached, carrying a chisel and a hammer. From afar it looked like the man wore several thick bracelets, but when he stood closer Akash saw that both of his forearms were striped with bulging scars. "This one is new." Kumar-ji pointed to Akash. "Tell him the rules and give him what he needs to do the job." The man bowed toward Kumar-ji, who turned and walked back toward the jeep.

"Pay attention!" The man squatted down on the other side of the stone block, took a square piece of cardboard, and held it against the stone. He etched the outline of the template onto the block. In the grip of the man's large hands the tools looked like toys. Akash tried not to stare at the thick scars, wondering how the man had been injured. "You need to first break the big rocks into pieces and then make the pieces fit this size." The man spoke loudly, looking at Akash as if he had already run out of patience.

"This is how you should hold the hammer." He placed the chisel on top of one of the lines he had drawn and pounded it down with the hammer. After only a few strong hits a piece broke off. "Then you take the small piece and shape it into a cube like this." He pointed to a small pyramid of stone cubes piled up behind Akash. "They need to look like those." The man stood up and straightened his back. "You only get paid for perfect ones."

The man left before Akash could ask any questions. It had looked easy when the man had split the stone. Akash positioned himself in front of the block and aligned the chisel with the marking. He let the hammer fall onto the chisel, but the chisel scraped off to the side, not even scratching the stone. He tried again, this time putting more force behind the hammer, and a small piece split off the stone's surface. Akash concentrated on keeping the chisel at the same spot each time he pounded the hammer until a small hair-thin crack grew down from its tip. One more hit and the block was split. He picked up the smaller piece and held it against one of the cubes from the pyramid.

"You need to hold it with your feet." A boy about his own age sat down next to Akash. The boy grabbed the piece of stone and held it between his feet like a monkey. Then he began to chisel away small chunks by expertly adjusting the angle of the tools until one side of the cube was straight. He turned the stone without using his hands. "You see?" Akash nodded. He wouldn't be able to do it as quickly as the boy, but he understood the technique. "What's your name?" the boy asked. "I'm Anant."

"Akash. Thank you for helping me."

"Stay away from him!" Anant pointed in the direction of the man who had given Akash the hammer and chisel. "We call him 'the Tiger' because of his scars. He is the foreman. He sees and knows everything!"

"How did he get the scars?"

"I don't know."

"Why are you working here?" Akash asked.

"My family used to come to the quarry every year to work. We would just go home to our village during the monsoon season, when the mine is closed. But my father had an accident and can't work anymore, and my mother is sick. So they had to borrow money from Kumar-ji and sent me to work alone this year. I came back early, since it hardly rained."

"How much do you earn?" Akash had placed the next stone between his feet and tried to hit the chisel the way Anant had shown him.

"I earn eighty rupees a day, about two thousand a month," Anant said. "I can break up about seventy stones a day."

"When do we get paid?"

"On Friday afternoons we go to the main office and they look in their books to find how much money we get for the week, and they write down how much we still owe."

"How much does your family owe?"

"My family owes forty thousand rupees," Anant said. "Kumar-ji's son keeps track of the debt in the ledger. He just subtracts the money you earn from your family's debt. They also take out what you owe the quarry for food, tools, and such. I always take a small amount in cash for myself to buy *chai* or sweets."

"I'm thirsty." Akash wiped the sweat from his face.

"Here." Anant offered him a plastic bottle. "You should keep one of these with you at all times. You can refill it over there." He pointed in the direction of a low, flat-roofed building on the far end of the quarry. Akash took a sip of the stale water. "It's a little dusty, but you get used to it," Anant said.

"The water?" Akash asked.

"No, the work," Anant said. Akash knew he would never get used to it.

12

In the evening a siren howled, signaling the end of the workday.

"Come! I'll show you around before we go to get food. The line is shorter later," Anant said.

It felt good to walk. Akash's back hurt and he examined the palms of his hands, where blisters were beginning to form.

"Once you are over the blisters your hands get hard. Your back also gets used to it after a while," Anant said.

"What's that?" Akash pointed to a raised causeway cutting through the flat desert landscape behind the far end of the quarry.

"That's the railway track. The express train to

and from Delhi passes here twice a day. Two tracks cross, so the train slows down. You can hear its whistle late in the evenings and before noon."

They turned and walked past a line of workers streaming toward the food tent as Anant led the way up a hill of gravel that looked down on a row of flat-roofed buildings. "This is where the blacksmiths make the tools," Anant said.

"What is he doing?" Akash pointed to a boy who was tied next to a wheel that he turned with one arm.

"This wheel fans air to the blacksmith's fire," Anant said. "That's where the Tiger puts you when he catches you."

"Catches you doing what?"

"When you crack slabs of stones that are already cut to size, or when you take overlong breaks. Or sometimes he just makes a kid work the wheel because he feels like it."

"How come the boy is still working? I thought the siren marked the end of the workday," Akash asked.

"The Tiger has his own hours. He decides when the boy can stop," Anant said.

⌊...⌉

After their evening meal Anant had invited Akash to sleep in his hut. What Anant called a hut was more like a windowless tomb made of uneven bricks and cobblestones covered with three slabs of stone standing in a row of similar makeshift shelters. "It protects me from rain, sun, and sandstorms," Anant explained. They placed a second charpoy next to Anant's, leaving just enough space on the floor for their water bottles and tools. Akash put his bag next to him on the bed and asked, "How long have you worked in the quarry since you came this time?"

Anant took a moment before he answered. "I don't remember." He shrugged. "I stopped counting the days."

Akash decided to cut notches into the frame of his charpoy for each day he stayed at the quarry. It was important to count.

13

The next day they sat down at the same spot and began chiseling the slabs into cubes. By noon Akash had lined up a row of cobblestones and in his mind he added up his earnings. The work was boring. He tried to focus on a spot in the distance until it melted into a mirage like he used to see when he was taking a break from tending the fields, but every time he tried to stare into space for a while to let his mind escape into a dream he heard the Tiger threatening. Akash looked at the slab he was about to divide into four stones, each of them one fourth of the original. If he continued to divide one of those stones in half, he would get two eighths. The eighths could be cut into sixteenths, the sixteenths into thirty-seconds. In his mind Akash continued to divide the stone into smaller and smaller fractions. Which would be the smallest possible number? Akash paused. The denominators were getting larger but the fractions were getting smaller and smaller. There was no end to this series of numbers. It would go on indefinitely. He wanted to lie on his back, close his eyes, and follow the pull toward the infinite. Akash had taken imaginary trips to this void before when looking up at the night sky, following countless stars, envisioning the endless cosmos.

"Hey." Anant startled him out of his thoughts. "You need to keep chipping away, or the Tiger will come after you!"

"I know," Akash said, shaking his head to clear his mind. He took the slab and began to chisel it into two halves.

"What are you thinking about?"

"Oh, I miss going to school," Akash said. "Don't you miss it?"

"No," Anant said. "I only went to school for a short time, back when I still lived in our village. The teacher didn't always come, and when he was there he hit us with a stick. We had to sit on the floor and memorize things. I like working here better. No one beats me and I even get paid."

Akash tried to concentrate on the stone in front of him.

"Can you read?" Anant asked.

Akash nodded. He placed another finished stone on his tray before he got up to pull the next slab closer. After he had worked enough to pay back what his family owed Kumar-ji he would return to school. But how long would it take to work off his family's debt?

"What is it like?"

"What?"

"Reading."

"It's like going to different places without leaving where you are," Akash said. He remembered his morning lessons with Mr. Sudhir, how much he had loved the short exercises in English and, of course, the math. How could Dadima be so cruel as to send him to work in the quarry? His anger hissed like the raised head of a cobra. Uncle Jagdish was her older son. He should be taking care of the family now. Akash had seen how it could be done. A neighbor had taken the money for the *bhukki* away from his son.

For what seemed to be a long time Akash's family had overheard their arguments and the son's wailing as if he were in horrible pain. Then one day he went back to work, looking older and gaunt, but strong enough to help in the field.

"Careful!" Anant startled Akash out of his thoughts. "You shouldn't hit too hard. Then the stone splits the wrong way and the slab is ruined!"

"I know." Akash wiped the sweat from his forehead and took a deep breath.

Maybe this was the punishment he had to endure for not listening to Bapu about the tortoise. Maybe the gods were testing his strength. Akash would show them that he was worthy of their support.

14

There is Badri, Kumar's son." Anant pointed to the man seated in the front of the room. Akash and Anant had stood in line for their weekly payment for a long time. The line had started near the food tent and slowly crept its way to the main building. Kumar's son sat on a swivel chair behind a desk with the drawer half open. His white kurta bulged over his well-fed belly. One of his pudgy hands rested on the thick ledger in which he wrote a sum for everyone who approached him from the queue. On his other hand, lying atop the armrest of the chair, a red stone set in a broad golden ring sparkled.

"Can I see the book?" Akash had finally made it

to the front of the line. He and Anant had waited for over an hour to receive their pay.

"Why?"

"I just want to see it."

"Can you even read?"

"A little bit."

With his swollen fingers Kumar's son turned the book around before he waved to a skinny boy with a tray to bring him tea. Akash recognized his name at the top of the page.

"Is this how much my family owes?" he asked.

Kumar's son took a noisy sip from his tea before he nodded. "Yes."

"That's 450,000 rupees?"

"If that's what the book says, that's how much you owe."

"How much did I make this week?"

"450 rupees."

"But I earn eighty rupees a day. That's 560 rupees for seven days."

Badri frowned and bent forward. A wad of damp black hair peeked out from under his collar. "You think food and tools are free?"

"What's this number?" Akash pointed to the second column.

"That is the interest we charge."

"You are adding 20 percent interest to the debt at the end of every month?"

"Are you trying to be smart?" Badri pulled the ledger back to his side of the desk. "Maybe I should tell the foreman."

"Is this Anant's page?" Akash stretched himself to point to the column near the right margin. Badri nodded. "Other people are waiting. Do you want to take out some money or not?"

"Yes," Akash said, and held up his hand for Badri to place a hundred-rupee note onto his palm. He had seen the amount of debt stated in the column for the end of the month. The number was bigger than the debt at the beginning of the month.

15

What do you mean? I don't understand." Anant looked confused after Akash had told him what he had seen in Badri's ledger.

"Our families' debts will not get smaller. The pay we receive for our work doesn't even maintain the amount they currently owe." Akash had written the calculation on a page in his notebook and showed it to Anant. But Anant just shook his head.

"You will not be able to leave anytime soon. We will have to stay until a very good harvest would allow our families to reduce their debt substantially. Until then we are kept here like prisoners," Akash said. The night was clear and stars speckled the black sky. They sat outside Anant's hut in the pale light of an almost full moon, the piles of cobblestones and mounds of boulders looking like the surface of a distant planet.

"What do you want to do?" Anant asked.

"We have to leave," Akash said.

"Where do you want to go?"

Akash shrugged. "I don't know."

"I don't want to go anywhere," Anant said. "Here I have enough food. Nobody beats me, and I can visit my family during the monsoon."

Akash shook his head. "I can't stay here," he said quietly.

"Will you go back to your family?"

"No." Akash called out the word louder than he had intended. "My Dadima gave me away like the runt of a litter. If I went back there she would turn me right around."

"But don't you feel bad about leaving them?"

"Did she feel bad about sending me here?" Akash asked, shooting Anant an angry glance.

"Where else would you go? And how would you get there? You can't just walk out the front gate," Anant said.

"Didn't you say that the train to Delhi slows down behind the quarry at night?"

"Yes. In about an hour you will hear the whistle."

Akash thought about his idea.

"Do you know anyone in Delhi?" Anant asked.

"No."

"What will you do once you get there?"

"I don't know. But there has to be a better way than this," Akash said. He got up. "You sure you don't want to come with me?"

Anant nodded. "I want to stay."

"I can't," said Akash, and stepped inside the hut to fetch his bag.

16

He could feel the vibration on the tracks before he saw the light in the distance. When the train slowed down with a loud screech Akash held his ears shut. He flattened himself against the ground beside the track and waited until the train came to a complete halt before he got up and opened the door closest to him. The wagon was painted light blue on the outside and on a wooden sign he read AJMER–DELHI. The door opened easily and he climbed up the metal stairs.

This was his first time on a train. Akash stood in a small corridor in front of a door with a tinted glass window. He hoped it would lead to a compartment where he could hide under a bench. But on entering he found himself in the brightly lit aisle between rows of upholstered seats occupied by white-skinned foreigners. He had seen white people before, but he couldn't help staring at the woman in the front row. Her hair was the color of egg yolk, cropped short like a man's, and her skin white as milk, speckled with light brown dots. He clenched his bag, trying to balance against the sudden movement as the train came back to life, but he stumbled and fell against the woman's shoulder. She pulled away from him with a squeal. The man who sat beside her leaned over and shoved Akash back into the aisle. They both looked at him with a mix of pity and disgust, as if he were a dog infested with disease. Akash found his balance and quickly walked through the aisle, careful not to touch anyone. There was music in the car, Rajasthani music, the kind his neighbors performed during festivals. He recognized a song but could not make out where the music came from. He reached the door at the other end of the compartment and pulled it open. It led to a small corridor separating two doors labeled TOILET WESTERN STYLE and TOILET INDIAN STYLE. He wondered if the toilet would be a good place to hide. Maybe the tourists would not use the Indian-style toilet. He needed to find a hiding place quickly. Through another glass door he could see a man in a blue uniform coming up the aisle toward him. The passengers handed him papers. When the ticket controller checked the last row of passengers, Akash pressed down the handle on the door with the INDIAN STYLE sign, but it was locked. He would be caught! But just as the man in the blue uniform turned to open the glass door to enter the corridor, Akash felt a hand on his shoulder, pulling him backward into a dark space.

17

You can come out now, boy." The man shifted his legs aside to let Akash climb out from beneath the shelf he had been shoved under. "What's your name?"

"Akash." He hadn't noticed the man in a niche opposite the toilets. He sat on a stool squeezed between the wall and the shelf, operating a black machine with buttons and dials.

"I am Lal Singh, tape recorder operator on the Shatabdi Express. I change the music tapes for the first- and second-class compartments. And I thought you needed some help before the ticket controller came."

"Thank you for helping me," Akash said, as he

stepped out into the narrow corridor to stretch himself. Lal Singh had a smooth face, round as a roti. His hair was slicked back and shimmered in the light from the single bulb dangling from above. The rolled-up sleeves of his shirt exposed hairless forearms as soft as a baby's thighs. On the wall behind him Akash saw a large poster.

"Do you like Hrithik Roshan?" Lal Singh asked. Akash recognized the actor. The poster showed the young man in tight white jeans, his muscular upper body clad only with a sleeveless vest, flexing his pronounced stomach muscles. He held his arms stretched out and thrust his hips forward. Akash shrugged. He didn't like this actor more than any other. "He was in *Krrish*. Did you see that film?"

In Akash's village only the electro-wallah, who knew how to repair electric things, had owned a television. Sometimes Ravi and Akash had watched a movie from a distance on his TV. "I don't know," Akash said.

"You would remember if you had seen him," Lal Singh said disapprovingly. "Look at these muscles." Lal Singh's short finger gently touched the photo. "And you know what this is?" He pointed to the actor's right hand.

"It's his hand." Akash knew he was supposed to give a different answer.

"He has a disfigured thumb. When he was a child the doctors told him he could never dance, but he proved them wrong. It is a sign that he is loved by the gods." Lal Singh pulled Akash back into the niche for a closer look at the poster. "See!" It looked as if two thumbs had grown together, like a gnarl on a tree branch. A heavy sweet smell filled Akash's nostrils as he bent closer toward Lal Singh, who tenderly stroked the poster. A sudden sideways movement of the train threw Akash against Lal Singh's soft thighs and hips. Lal Singh turned and smiled, his cheeks forming two doughy balls. Akash withdrew until his back pressed against the opposite wall of the corridor, leaving ample space between himself and Lal Singh.

"Where are you from?" Akash didn't want to talk about the actor anymore.

"I'm from Delhi. I have worked for the railway for twelve years. My father just retired after thirty-six years in the railway service. Good work!"

Lal Singh's eyes scanned Akash from head to toe. "What will you do in the city?"

"I'm meeting my father." The lie came easily

from Akash's lips. "My Bapu works there and he has sent for me."

"What does your Bapu do?"

"He is a *mazdur*. He works on construction sites."

"But when he sent for you he didn't send any money for a train ticket, ha?"

Akash felt a hot surge rise from his chest. He looked out the window, where the darkness was interrupted by a faint glow of lights in the distance. Then he was startled by a shrill woman's voice announcing over the loudspeaker that they would soon arrive at a station.

"You can do me a favor now," Lal Singh said.

"What do you want me to do?"

"You can buy me tea and samosa when we get to the next stop."

⌊...⌉

Lal Singh had given him two ten-rupee notes and he had received five one-rupee coins back for change. Now Akash was balancing the two low cups of hot tea in his hands. He had wrapped the samosa in a piece of paper and held it with his elbow pressed against his hip. But when he approached the train Akash couldn't remember which car he had stepped out of. Each of the wagons looked the same to him. He asked a skinny porter in a red jacket, who pointed him in the direction of the first-class car.

"I thought you'd come back," Lal Singh said when he saw Akash. "You wouldn't want to leave your book with me." Akash's bag sat on Lal Singh's lap and he waved the textbook in his hands. "So you're studying English?" He laughed and his jowls quivered as he stuffed the book back in the sack. Akash passed him the tea and the samosa. He clenched his bag under his arm and wished he hadn't left it inside the train. He would need to remember to carry it with him at all times.

"I'm trying to improve my English," he said, looking down at the grimy linoleum floor.

"And that's why you're meeting your *mazdur* father in Delhi?" Lal Singh took a bite of the samosa. Akash squatted down, leaning against the wall. His mouth watered as he watched Lal Singh chew. His empty stomach growled. The tea was hot and scalded his throat.

"I will help him earn money," Akash said. Lal Singh licked his greasy fingers. The train began to move, and soon they had left the station and only darkness rushed by on the other side of the window.

"The controller will come again to ask the new passengers for their tickets," Lal Singh said. "You should crawl under the shelf. I'll take a nap. The next tape will play for over an hour, so we can both take a little snooze." Akash crawled under the shelf, trying to find space for his legs. Soon he heard Lal Singh snore; his upper body slumped against the tape recorder.

Akash thought about Anant and wondered if he should have stayed. Then Akash reminded himself of the amount he had seen written in the ledger, and that even if he had stayed, he would have never been able to earn enough to pay off his family's debt. The anger flickered again and he knew that it had been the right decision to leave the quarry. But when he tried to imagine what would await him in Delhi, there was only a hollow fear. He reached into his bag and pulled out the picture of Saraswati. It was too dark under the shelf to see her, but he put her image on his lap, brought his hands together in front of his chest, and asked for her help.

Akash woke up feeling Lal Singh's fingers tickling the nape of his neck.

"We're almost there!" he said. When Akash climbed out from under the shelf Lal Singh adjusted himself on the stool and blocked Akash's way out of the niche. The loudspeaker crackled again and the voice announced their arrival in Delhi.

"You could stay with me," Lal Singh said. "In case your father doesn't come. I live in a flat behind Pahar Ganj just a short walk from the train station. We could watch movies together." He breathed heavily.

It was tempting to go with the only person he knew in Delhi. Akash had no clear idea what he would do when he arrived at the train station. But Lal Singh stared at him the way a cat looked before it pounced on a mouse. Akash could feel Lal Singh's damp hand on the small of his back, slowly moving closer toward his buttocks. He pushed his way passed Lal Singh.

"No," he said. "I'm sure I'll find my father." The train slowed down and a group of red-vested porters stormed into the corridor, rushing to the tourist compartment. Akash quickly slipped around them, eager to reach the door.

18

Akash jumped down from the train into a churning sea of people, some of them carrying heavy loads, others following skinny red-vested coolies, with suitcases or bundles on their heads. A train rolled in along the other bank of the platform, its decreasing speed accompanied by a screeching noise. It stopped with a loud sigh and people poured out of its doors.

Akash's nostrils were clogged with the acrid stench of the city. He couldn't identify its origin, but it stung his eyes and left a burning sensation in his throat. For a moment he stood still, uncertain where to go; then with a shove from a shoulder or a bag he found himself in the stream moving toward the broad steel staircase that took passengers to the overpass that led over the tracks to the main building. He ducked aside, leaned against a pillar, and stared at the moving masses. A whistle blew and the train on the opposite side of the platform started to move. Men hung from the doors. Hands waved from the windows. Soon the train in which Akash had arrived began to roll away. He watched its two back lights disappear in the distance and swallowed hard to wash away the salty taste of tears that lined the back of his throat.

He had to find a place to sleep. A little farther down the platform he saw a building. Two doors opened to brightly lit toilet stalls. Akash entered and took a drink from the faucet of the filthy sink. Mosquitoes danced in front of the flickering fluorescent tube that hung above a stained mirror. He rubbed water over the black down that had grown back on his skull and returned to the platform. The stream of people had not lessened, though, according to the large clock hanging from one of the girders, it was past midnight. Akash walked to the end of the platform, stepping carefully around several men who had stretched out on the concrete to sleep. A dog had followed him and looked up at Akash before turning three times and lying down with a sigh. Akash sat down and traced the braids formed by the tracks until they vanished in the darkness. Heavy from exhaustion, he slowly curled up like a cashew. But he couldn't sleep. It was too unsettling to lie alone among strangers. Instead, he rolled on his back, pulled his legs up, and stared into the sky. The city's haze didn't allow a clear view of the stars and the moon was a pale, milky stain behind a dirty curtain. Akash listened to the unfamiliar sounds and felt a sudden longing for home. He remembered how he and Bapu had slept outside when the nights got too hot. He missed the familiar sound of Bapu's snoring and the frantic buzzing of the cicadas. But he couldn't go home. He forced himself to remember the promise he had made to himself in the temple after the thirteenth-day ceremony. He thought of his father's words: *What you desire is on its way.* He would find the way to reach his goal. Akash got up again and walked toward the back of the toilet building. Faint light fell on a large, empty cardboard box under the window. Akash crawled inside and closed the lid.

19

He woke up from a sharp pain in his side. The policeman's face was dark, but Akash could see his teeth and the whites of his eyes gleaming. "Hey! Get up!" the policeman yelled, and let his stick come down again, this time on Akash's shoulder. Another sharp pain.

"What are you doing here?" The policeman used the stick now to poke Akash in the ribs.

"I'm sleeping," Akash said, eyeing the stick as he crawled out of the box.

"Come with me to the station! We'll take care of you there!" He pulled on Akash's shoulder.

"Please! Leave me alone!" Akash held his right hand up to defend himself against the next strike.

"What's in your bag?" The policeman grabbed the bag and pulled out the English textbook.

"It's just a book!" Akash trembled. The policeman held the book in his hands and studied the title. "English? Where did you steal it?"

"I didn't steal it!"

"Come! You can tell me more at the station!"

"I can't go to the station. I'm waiting for my Bapu!"

"So your Bapu lets you sleep alone in the train station. You kids all think we are stupid." The policeman gripped Akash's shoulder and pulled him up. "Let's go!"

"I can pay you. If you let me stay!"

The policeman let go of Akash and frowned at him. "How much do you have?" Akash opened his shirt pocket and pulled out the bill. "One hundred rupees."

The policeman snatched the money. "This only buys you two days," he said. "If I see you after that I'll take you to the station."

⌊⋯⌉

The sky finally grew pale. Akash sat beside the cardboard box, his rib cage throbbing from the policeman's blow. He was thirsty and his stomach grumbled. He went to the toilet for water, but now a man sat on a stool at the entrance holding his hand out. "Five rupees!" he demanded. Akash backed away.

The platform was still filled with people rushing in all directions. An old man offered samosas from a pushcart. The triangular pastries were filled with potato, peas, cauliflower, and spices. They shone yellow-gold. The cart owner fished another load out of the bubbling oil. With a slotted spoon he drained the grease before he placed them onto the heap. Akash stepped closer. His mouth watered as the smell filled his nostrils. The man looked at him. "How many do you want?" But Akash only shook his head and walked on.

He stopped in front of a large signboard. In white letters it announced the names of trains—Punjab Mail, Jhelum Express, Shatabdi, Shiv Ganga— followed by their arrival and departure times and their final destinations. Every line began with a four-digit identification number for each of the announced trains. The identification number for the Shatabdi Express was 1788. Akash added the digits $1 + 7 + 8 + 8 = 24$. Then his mind began to find the possible combinations to reach 24 through adding, subtracting, multiplying, or dividing. This used to be a game he played with himself during boring hours at school. There were fifteen possible ways to reach 24:

$$9 \times (7 + 1) / 3 = 24$$
$$9 \times 8 / 3 = 24 \ldots$$

For a moment he felt relief, as if he had met old friends who assured him that all would be fine. But finding all possible equations to reach 24 did not fill his stomach.

A voice from the loudspeaker announced the arrival of a train from Mumbai on platform 8. As soon as the train had stopped, four boys, not older than Akash, scurried against the current of departing passengers and jumped, quick as chipmunks, up the three metal stairs before disappearing inside a first-class compartment. Through the smudged window Akash could see their silhouettes moving from one row to the next. Their shadows passed into the next car. As quickly as they had jumped inside they now tumbled down the stairs, each carrying a plastic sack. Two of the boys hurried toward the magazine stand in the middle of the platform. They looked like brothers, thin and very dark-skinned. The taller of the two pulled newspapers and magazines out of the sacks and offered them to the man behind the stand, who inspected them, nodded, and gave the boys each a bill. The third boy wore a red scarf around his neck and carried a bulging sack from which several plastic bottles stuck out. While waiting for the other two, he shared the contents of a biscuit box with the fourth boy before tossing the package onto the tracks.

When the next train stopped and the passengers had melted into the stream of people on the platform, Akash pushed himself against the current and slid into a third-class compartment. The seats were only wooden benches and the windows had no glass, just bars. He crawled under the first row. A shiny piece of paper caught his eye. He crawled closer, but it was only an empty candy wrapper. In a corner, where the linoleum was tucked against the side wall of the compartment, a rupee coin shimmered. He snatched it, though one rupee would not even buy him a samosa. Under the next bench he collected a bag of potato chips with some crumbs inside and two empty water bottles. With a sudden start the train began to move. Akash hurried to the exit. Before the train gained speed he jumped off and landed hard on the platform. He had stuck the two plastic bottles into his bag and emptied the contents of the potato chip bag into his mouth, letting the crumbs melt into a salty and greasy clump before he swallowed. Suddenly, three of the four boys he had watched collecting garbage blocked his way. The tallest of the three pointed to his bag and said, "This is our garbage!"

20

Akash pulled the two bottles out of his bag. The tall boy grabbed them and dropped them into the large sack he wore around his shoulder. "What else do you have in there?" the tall boy asked, and pulled Akash's bag. Akash didn't want to lose Bapu's shawl and the book and notebook he was carrying. He stumbled backward but he wouldn't let go of the bag. The second boy called, "You are working in our territory. Go and find a different platform!" and struck Akash in the ribs with a fist. As Akash bent over to protect himself against further jabs he heard a voice. "Leave him alone!" Akash looked up into the face of the boy with the red scarf and straightened himself, clutching the bag.

The other boys stepped back, but continued to glare at Akash. The boy who had given the order was about his own age. His clothes were cleaner and fit better than those of the other three. But his upper lip melted into a thick scar that led up to his nose, giving him a rabbitlike expression. "What's your name?" Rabbit-boy asked Akash. His voice sounded as if he were pinching his nose. Akash answered.

"Why have you come to Delhi?"

For a moment Akash thought he would tell the same lie he had told Lal Singh and the policeman. But then he remembered how it hadn't served him well the last two times he claimed his father would pick him up.

"I came to see the Taj Mahal."

The boys laughed. Akash didn't know he had said something funny.

"The Taj Mahal is in Agra. That's a five-hour train ride from Delhi," Rabbit-boy said, and reached for Akash's bag. "What's in there?"

Akash pulled away but said, "A math notebook. I like math." Akash prepared himself for another shower of laughter. But Rabbit-boy silenced the others with a disapproving glance.

"You are good with numbers?"

Akash nodded, waiting for the joke Rabbit-boy would make at his expense. Instead, the boy remained serious.

"How good?"

Akash shrugged. "I can add, subtract, multiply, and divide quickly."

"In your head?"

"Yes."

Rabbit-boy looked intently at Akash, as if he were carefully considering Akash's answers. The others seemed to have lost interest. The dark-skinned boys began to count the bottles in their sacks, accompanied by the shortest boy's humming.

Rabbit-boy pulled a paper out of his pocket and unfolded it.

"How much is 12 times 11?"

"132," Akash said.

"8 times 9?"

"72."

The boy turned the paper around. "How much is 20 percent of 170?"

"34," Akash said without hesitation, wondering why the boy was carrying a sheet with multiplication and percentage tables in his pocket.

Rabbit-boy folded the paper back into a small square. "How did you learn to do this?"

"I went to school in my village and it just comes easily to me."

"It doesn't come easily to *me*. Numbers just skitter away from me like chipmunks," Rabbit-boy said, his voice lower. "What a gift you have!"

"Can I stay with you on the platform for a while? I could help you with math, if you'd like me to." He wondered what kind of math a boy needed to live in the train station.

Rabbit-boy smiled. "My name is Rohit." Rohit pointed to the boys. "These are Sunil, Deepak, and his brother, Mandeep. But we call him Madhup." The small boy looked like he had just woken up. His eyelids drooped over his eyes. When his name was called he started to hum like his namesake, *madhup*, the bee, nodding his head slowly. His brother, Deepak, tugged his arm and the humming stopped.

"Where are you from?" Rohit asked.

"I'm from Rajasthan, not far from Jodhpur."

"I'm a desert boy too! Ajmer district. My family lives near Pushkar." Rohit patted Akash on the shoulder and said in his nasal voice, "You should stay with us."

21

Akash followed the boys across the tracks to the low end of platform 1. A stray dog perched on top of a heap of garbage, chewing on what could have been chicken skin or the sole of a sandal. Another dog steadied a small rectangular aluminum container with its paw before attacking its corners with frantic licks. Crows picked at two stained napkins. The smell was overbearing and Akash forced himself to breathe through his mouth. "This is where they throw out the leftovers from the luxury trains. It's a good place to find food." Rohit picked up what looked to Akash like a lump of greasy paper, pulled off the wrapping, and broke a fried potato cutlet in two. "Here," Rohit said. "Have some breakfast." Akash hastily swallowed the mushy potatoes. Dadima used to tell him not to eat anything from the floor. Now he was scavenging through heaps of garbage to find food.

"Look at this." Rohit was holding two small boxes of thin cardboard in his hand.

"What's this?" Akash asked.

"The foreigners eat it for breakfast. They soak it in milk," Rohit explained, passing one of the small boxes to Akash. In red letters the words CORN FLAKES were written on the front of the box. Akash opened his and tried one of the flakes. They tasted like potato chips without salt.

"We go through this heap several times a day to collect food and plastic. You can get fourteen rupees per kilo for empty water bottles," Rohit said.

Akash kept an eye on the dogs as he waded through the garbage, turning over containers, rummaging through plastic bags and wrappings. He knew to be careful with meat. A piece of chicken, left in one of the small aluminum boxes, looked tempting, but the skin glistened suspiciously and smelled rotten. With his fingers Akash scraped the rice and lentils out and quickly swallowed the mash. Flies kept landing on his face and head, their buzzing a constant nuisance. He found several bottles and placed them in his bag before they left the garbage pile to walk up the stairs to the overpass.

"Now we'll show you where we get the money for the bottles," Rohit said, leading the group away from the slum and toward a row of higher buildings, each crowned with a dirty billboard announcing a different business. They turned the corner at Puja Electronics and came to a narrow alley where huge tubs filled with plastic bottles were lined against the wall. A ladder was leaned against one of the tubs, and a boy performed a strange dance on top of the bottles in an effort to crush them down.

"Give your bag to Prithviraj," Rohit said, dumping his sack in front of a man who was sitting on a red plastic chair between two of the tubs.

Prithviraj placed the bag onto a scale. "Just about one kilo," he said, and handed Akash fourteen rupees. Next he weighed the contents of Rohit's bag. When Prithviraj leaned back and announced, "Two and a half kilograms," Rohit quickly turned around to pull out the paper from his pocket that he had used to quiz Akash earlier. "Thirty-five rupees," Prithviraj said. "That's correct," Akash whispered in Rohit's ear. "You don't need to check it."

"Let me show you a trick," Akash said as they were waiting for the others' bottles to be weighed.

"What kind of trick?"

"A trick that helps you multiply numbers."

"Well, okay," Rohit said, his forehead frowning skeptically.

"If you want to multiply single-digit numbers, like 7 times 8, you first ask yourself how much is missing from each number until you get to ten."

"What do you mean?"

"How much is 10 minus 7?"

"3."

"Good. How much is 10 minus 8?"

"2."

"Perfect! Now you write the numbers like this," Akash said, and wrote on a scrap of paper with a pencil stub he had found in the garbage:

7 3

8 2
___

"Are you following so far?"

Rohit nodded. "Now you subtract diagonally: 7 minus 2 to get 5. That is the first digit of your answer. Then you multiply vertically: 3×2 to get 6.

That is the second digit of the product. The answer is 56!"

Rohit studied the calculation.

"Now you do it. Multiply 8 times 8." Akash handed Rohit paper and pencil.

"There are two missing to get to 10 from 8."

Rohit wrote

$$8 \quad 2$$
$$\underline{8 \quad 2}$$

on the paper.

"Excellent! The rule is called 'Vertically and Crosswise.' What do you do next?"

"I multiply 2 by 2 to get the first number."

"Yes, you multiply them, but that gives you the second number," Akash said. "Go on."

"8 minus 2 is 6," Rohit said slowly. "The total is 64."

"Yes! You see how simple this is!" Akash beamed at Rohit.

"Not really," he said. "You can do it in your head. I can't. I think I'll stick with the little paper in my pocket."

Akash shrugged. "It is really fascinating. These rules come from ancient Vedic scriptures. My old teacher used to teach me those. They give you lots of shortcuts for mental math."

"It's still mental math," Rohit said. "I don't like it." He crumbled the paper into a ball and flicked it away.

22

Where is he going to sleep?" Sunil asked on their way back to the train station.

"Maybe Ramesh will like his story," Rohit said.

"But he only takes one boy and that's you."

"I told you I will be leaving soon. So he'll need another boy," Rohit answered.

"I wish he'd take me. Sleeping on top of Ramesh-ji's stall is so much safer than hiding in the gap between the roof and the overpass," Sunil said.

"Ramesh-ji doesn't like thieves," Rohit answered. "That's why he doesn't let you stay with him."

"Who is Ramesh?" Akash asked.

"Ramesh-ji is the magazine-wallah who lets me sleep on the roof of his stall on platform 8 at night.

I give him money every week for a place to sleep and for the police."

"You give money to the police?" Akash remembered the policeman who had beaten him the other night.

"You don't pay *hafta*, you get their *lathi*," Deepak said, suddenly breaking into what Akash believed to be a movie song, accompanied by an exaggerated dance, shimmying his shoulders back and forth. He swung an imaginary stick in the air, then turned sideways, straightened himself like a soldier, and saluted the others with two fingers of his right hand.

"Stop pretending to be Shotgun Sinha. You need his scar and his mustache," Sunil said, laughing, pretending to flatten an imaginary mustache with his index fingers. "And a better voice," Rohit said.

Rohit led Akash toward the bookstall near one of the broad staircases on platform 8. It was shaped like a box made from red bricks, with a rectangular opening, and was not much bigger than the stone hut Anant had shared with Akash at the quarry.

"Ramesh-ji, meet Akash!" A wiry old man perched on a high stool behind the counter looked up from the book he was reading, his short hair a thatch of white. "I found Akash on the platform today. He arrived from a place not too far from Ajmer."

Newspapers in different Indian languages were displayed on stacks in front of him. Magazines hung from lines tied along the wall behind him, fastened neatly with clothespins, like rag towels. A broad shelf held several paperback books, and a small shrine with an idol of Hanuman, the monkey god, was erected in the corner. Ramesh stepped out of his stall, folded his hands in front of his chest, and nodded a *namaste*. Akash returned the greeting. He wondered if he should bend down to touch the older man's feet as he would have in his village. But since Rohit didn't perform this gesture of respect toward an elder, Akash also remained standing.

Ramesh was only a little taller than both boys and wore a spotlessly clean kurta that seemed to have been pressed just recently. His lined face was dominated by piercing, dark eyes that now were focusing their calm gaze on Akash.

"You take over for me, son. I will talk to your friend." Akash wondered how many times Rohit had brought boys to Ramesh asking for a place to stay. He felt anxious, as if he were going to take an exam he hadn't prepared for.

"Come on, boy," Ramesh said, motioning for Akash to follow him. "We'll walk a few steps to a quieter place." They sat down on one of the metal benches along the platform.

"Who died, son?"

Akash brushed his hand over his still very short hair. Only three weeks had passed since Bapu's death. "My father." Akash looked at his feet.

"Why did you leave your mother?"

"My mother died a long time ago." A large locomotive dappled with rust chugged by slowly, its screech forcing a short break in their conversation. When the locomotive had passed and the noise ebbed Ramesh turned to Akash. "What do you want to do in Delhi?"

"I want to find a real school where I can learn more math."

"Why did you leave your village?"

Rohit had mentioned that Ramesh chose boys according to their story. Akash didn't want to tell his, didn't want to recall his attempt to sell the tortoise, Bapu's death, and his short stay at the stone quarry, for fear that talking about them would make him relive the events and feel the pain again. But now Ramesh cocked his head and looked at him encouragingly. Akash took a deep breath and began, at first in a hesitating voice, then gaining assurance slowly, a trickle of words growing into a stream.

⌊…⌉

When he was done Akash felt surprisingly calm, like the still air after a storm had passed. Ramesh looked out at the platform and slowly bobbed his head before turning to Akash.

"Some children come here because they never felt at home in the family they were born into. I was one such." Ramesh's eyes were bright with memory, but before Akash could ask how Ramesh knew about feeling out of place in one's own family, the old man continued. "Rohit and the boys can show you how to make some money from selling plastic, but it won't be much. It will take you a while to achieve your goal."

"I know," Akash said, smiling. It was beginning to look like the old man would help him to stay.

"You are from the desert, aren't you?"

Akash nodded.

"Then you know that the fox needs patience to catch the *jird*."

In his mind he saw a brown desert mouse running away from a fox. Before he could come up with an answer Ramesh put his bony hand on Akash's knee. "You'll need protection from the police if you want to stay at the train station. I will let you sleep on my roof."

"Thank you." Ramesh had gotten up and Akash followed him back to the bookstall.

"I knew you would like him, Ramesh-ji," Rohit said.

"Did he show you where to wash?" Ramesh asked as he took his place behind the counter again.

Akash shook his head. "Not yet."

"You don't want to end up like those children over there." Ramesh pointed in the direction of a small girl with a baby hoisted on her hip. She wore a tattered skirt that dragged the floor. Her *lehnga* blouse might have been rose-colored once but now looked brown. Her face was covered with soot and the whites of her eyes stood out like two lights in the night. The baby's face was also filthy. The girl held up the palm of her hand in front of a woman in a sari to beg. "These children never wash. They carry disease. They die young," Ramesh-ji said. "You need to stay clean. It is the clean flower that makes the best honey!" Ramesh said, and turned his attention back to his book. Akash nodded and caught Rohit rolling his eyes.

23

This bridge connects the main station building with the platforms," Rohit explained as they walked across the overpass. "You can leave the station through the main building. But you cannot come back in unless you buy a ticket. If you want to get back in you have to climb over the low wall behind platform 14. Come, I'll show you."

They took the stairs leading to platform 14. This platform looked just like the one Akash had arrived on. Tracks on both sides, a toilet building, a juice vendor, a water fountain, and clusters of passengers either sitting on metal benches or huddling on the cement floor, waiting for their train. "This is the last railway line." Rohit pointed to the track to their left. "The New Delhi train station ends here."

Akash turned around. "Now I'll show you where we wash," Rohit said. "So you can be a *clean flower*, just as Ramesh-ji likes it." He rolled his eyes again and Akash had to laugh. They climbed swiftly over the low wall and reached a row of black, disheveled-looking huts with patched tin roofs. An open drain ran alongside the slanted makeshift structures, releasing an overpowering stench. A little girl squatted, lifted her skirt, and peed into the drain. "We get drinking water at the platforms, but this is where we wash," Rohit said, pointing to a hand-pump at the corner between two rows of the slum dwellings, where a fat woman worked the handle and water gushed into a plastic bucket. The woman chased off a skinny boy who was trying to redirect the stream of water onto his feet. To the side, an old man squatted against the brick wall in front of a steaming cauldron, stirring lumps of milk curd. A horde of flies swarmed on the rim of two dirty pots waiting beside him. After the fat woman had waddled away Rohit led Akash to the hand-pump, where they washed their hands in the dripping stream.

"Where are the others?"

"Deepak and Madhup are probably in the gap," Rohit said.

"The gap?"

"That's the space under the northern overpass on the roof of platform 3. They like to hang out there. Let's go. I'll show you."

They returned to platform 14 and walked up the staircase to the overpass. "You see, here," Rohit said as they had crossed the overpass and stood above platform 3. "This is where we have to climb through." Rohit ducked down to slip through a hole in the wire mesh that lined the fence along the overpass. "What are you doing?" Akash asked. "Jumping down on the roof. It's not very high," Rohit said before he let himself drop onto the corrugated plastic sheeting that covered the platform roof.

"Come!" Rohit called. Akash looked around to make sure no one was watching them before ducking down and following Rohit.

"Here you are," Rohit said. Deepak and Madhup, almost hidden from view, were sitting in the hollow between the roof and the overpass, leaning against a steel pillar with their eyes half closed. They each held a rag in front of their faces and inhaled.

"What are they doing?" Akash asked. He noticed a sharp smell, like gasoline.

"They are sniffing," Rohit answered.

"Sniffing what?"

"E-Raze! Cor-rec-tion fluid," Deepak answered, his voice slurred. "Even cheaper than glue. Same effect. Ahhhh!" He had lowered the rag.

"You want some? I have glue." Madhup offered Akash a small plastic bottle and his rag.

"No, thank you!" Akash turned to Rohit. "What does it do to them?"

"It makes them crazy," he answered.

"No, it makes us happy and not hungry!" Deepak called.

"It lets us forget things," Madhup added.

"After a while it ruins their brains. It is very dangerous," Rohit said.

Akash looked at the two, inhaling from their rags. *There are drugs here in the city as well*, Akash thought, and remembered Uncle Jagdish lying on his charpoy while Bapu worked in the field. *I will not let this happen to me.*

"Look! There is Sunil!" Rohit pointed to a group of tourists who were waiting for their train. "Watch this." Sunil walked slowly toward a woman who was carrying a small knapsack over her shoulder. Just as the train entered the station and the woman's attention was focused on finding the number of her compartment, Sunil slipped his hand into the pack, quickly pulled out her wallet, and ran away. "He is the master," Rohit said, raising his eyebrows in appreciation. Akash looked away. His new friends were thieves. They were inhaling chemicals and he would have to wade through garbage to find food and earn money. Akash could only stay in their company for a short time.

24

The next morning, Akash and Rohit were searching through a train compartment when it suddenly jerked into motion.

"What do we do now?" Akash asked. Usually, they ran outside before the doors would be shut. But this time Rohit just took a seat next to the window in the third-class compartment.

"We can't get out anymore," Akash said, watching the train gaining speed.

"We'll just sit here and enjoy the ride."

"But the train is moving."

"That's because it is going to Agra. Sit down!"

"But what if the ticket controllers come?"

"This is the last wagon of the train. His office is

in the front car," Rohit said. "It'll take him a while to get here. Don't worry."

Akash did worry. So far he had only collected garbage from trains as they were stopped in the station. Riding in a moving train brought back the bad memory of Lal Singh and his trip to New Delhi.

"You need to learn how to search moving trains before I leave."

"When are you going?" Akash sat down on the seat next to Rohit.

"I want to be back at home for Diwali."

"Why did you leave your family?"

"I have only my mother left. My father died and left her a widow just after I was born. She is ill and we need money for medicine."

"What kind of illness does she have?"

"We don't know exactly. Her fingers grew numb and she developed open wounds, first on her face, then on her hands and feet."

"Did she see a doctor?"

"The village healer came to our hut. He took one look at her and cried, 'Leprosy.' The word traveled like fire through the village. In the evening the head of the village elders came and asked us to move away."

"What do you mean, 'away'?"

"They thought she would be contagious and didn't want us near other people. I built a new hut made from reeds at the outskirts of the village and that's where we stayed for a while. I still worked as a cowherd. But she got worse. So I thought I could find money in the city." Rohit took a deep breath. "I have to hurry, though."

"Who is taking care of her while you are gone?"

"My aunt, her sister, lives at the other end of the village and leaves food and water for her. But she lives like an untouchable." Akash didn't know what to say. A silence settled between the boys. The lights leaped and flickered as the train clattered over a rail switch.

"My mother gave this to me." Rohit pointed to the red scarf he was wearing. "It brings me good luck."

"How long have you been gone?"

"I came right after Teej, during the month of Shravan. So it's been about two months," Rohit said.

Akash hoped he would not have to stay that long at the train station.

By now, the train had left the outskirts of New Delhi. For a while Akash looked out the window at the rushing blur of brown-and-yellow quilted fields interrupted by villages. At the next station a woman entered their compartment. She sat down near the window, two rows ahead, and placed a wire cage with several chickens on the empty seat beside her. The birds fluttered and cackled excitedly and small feathers twirled onto the floor.

"Did you always stay with Ramesh?"

"Not at first," Rohit said. "But he found me just as I was wondering if I could make it in the city. He is a good man."

"How about the others? Madhup, Deepak, and Sunil?"

"Deepak and Madhup came from Bihar with their parents, but they got lost in the turmoil of the train station."

"Their parents never came back to look for them?"

"It's hard to find someone in a huge city like Delhi. And, who knows, maybe their family didn't really miss them."

"How about Sunil?"

"He ran away from home after they beat him. He wants to go to Mumbai. His dream is to become an actor in Bollywood."

⌊...⌉

The train was back in motion. Rohit soon closed his eyes. Akash was afraid to sleep and kept glancing at the door to the compartment. Pursuing his goal would lead Rohit back to his village, but Akash could never go back. With a pang Akash remembered Anu. By now Kumar-ji would have told the family that Akash had run away. What had Anu thought when she heard what Akash had done? Would she understand? Akash imagined the letter he would write to her, describing the dread and hopelessness of the quarry and his escape by train. But Anu couldn't read. She would need to perform slave labor for Dadima until it was time for her to get married. Akash would not attend the wedding, but maybe there was a way to send a present later, when he had enough money.

⌊...⌉

"Here comes the ticket controller." Akash shook Rohit out of his sleep and pointed toward the door at the other end of the compartment. A man in a dark blue jacket had entered and stood in front of the passengers in the first berth. "Here, take this!" Rohit pulled a short broom out of his sack and handed it to Akash. "Just pretend you are a cleaner and he'll leave you alone."

Rohit pushed him into the aisle. "What will you do?" Akash whispered. The ticket controller was coming closer, but Rohit didn't answer. He just nodded and pointed to the broom. His face had taken on a strange expression. He looked like he was suddenly tired or had taken medication that made him very drowsy. Akash bent down and began to move the broom mechanically across the floor.

"Where is your ticket, son?" Akash heard the man address Rohit.

"I need to see your ticket!" The controller grew impatient and was shaking Rohit's shoulder. Rohit shrugged and made a gesture with his hands.

"You think I believe you when you pretend that you can't speak?"

"He was talking earlier." The woman with the chicken cage turned around and pointed to Akash. "With that one!"

A voice came over the loudspeaker announcing their arrival at the next station. The ticket controller's face flushed. The man jerked Rohit off the bench. "Maybe you'd like to explain your disability to the police at the next station." Rohit now hung in the man's grip like a doll. Akash turned around, still pretending to sweep the floor. He caught Rohit's eyes. Then he suddenly had an idea. With a quick movement he opened the wire cage and gave it a shake so the birds fluttered out. The woman started to scream and tried to catch the birds. The ticket controller let go of Rohit, who quickly ran toward the exit. Akash followed. "What are we going to do?"

"We'll jump off!" Rohit had pulled open the door. His hair stood up in the sudden breeze. The train had slowed down, the buildings gaining contour with the decreased speed. Akash turned around. "The ticket controller is coming after us!" he yelled against the noise of the train.

"You need to tuck your head in and try to roll on your shoulder!" Rohit called.

Akash saw the gray of the platform coming closer. He held his breath and jumped just a few seconds after Rohit, landing next to him on the hard cement.

"Are you all right?" Rohit stood up.

"Yes," Akash said. "My elbow hurts a bit, but I'm okay."

"I'm afraid we'll have to travel to the Taj Mahal some other day," Rohit said. "We have about two hours before the next train to Delhi stops here."

They walked through the station building and Rohit steered toward a group of taxi and three-wheeler drivers who were sitting next to their vehicles on the parking lot in front of the flat brick building, playing cards.

"Do you know *teen patti*?" Rohit asked.

"Yes," Akash said. "But I don't like to play."

"Doesn't your knowledge of math help you win card games?"

"No," Akash answered. "There is not much math in *teen patti*. You just hope that the cards you get are higher than the other players'. Since you don't get to change or trade cards there are no skills involved, just luck."

"Come on! Let's play some cards," Rohit insisted, and greeted one of the drivers like an old friend. Akash wondered how he could know people this far away from Delhi.

The men made space for Rohit and dealt him cards for the next round. Akash stood and observed them, thinking of Uncle Jagdish and how Dadima had given him the last rupees she should have paid Kumar-ji. The memory of his home in the village threw a dark shadow over his mood, and he suddenly longed to be alone. He bent down to Rohit and said, "I'll be waiting for you over by the entrance. I really don't want to play." As he walked away from the group he pulled an English-language newspaper from a trash can and sat down to read in English until it was time to take the train back to Delhi.

25

How did Saraswati decide when to help? What would he have to do to make Ganesha remove the obstacles from his path? Akash had woken early and was sitting up on the roof of Ramesh's magazine stall. This was already his third day in the train station. After he had bought food and paid Ramesh he had only fifty-five rupees left. Fifty-five was a triangular number. It used to calm him down to follow their intriguing sequence: 1, 3, 6, 10, 15, 21, 28, 36, 45, 55 . . . But now fifty-five just made him more restless. He could continue his math practice in his mind, but he wanted to sit at a desk, solving equations with paper and pencil. He wanted the challenge of working with someone who knew more than he did, or at least as much. Akash looked at Rohit, who was still wrapped in his blanket, breathing calmly in his sleep. Rohit would go back home soon, to help his mother. Rohit seemed to find humor in almost everything, wasn't weighed down by worries all the time like Akash. There had to be schools here in Delhi. Maybe he could enroll in a school or take the exam in Delhi. But how could he pay for a private school? Who would take a boy without parents or a proper home? How good did his results have to be to win a scholarship in a big city? These worries circled above him like vultures over carrion. Akash took his notebook out from under the shirt he used as a pillow and opened it to the page where he had placed the picture of Saraswati. He whispered his morning prayer: "I bow to Goddess Saraswati, who fulfills the wishes of the devotees. I pray she enlighten me with knowledge." *Help me soon*, he added.

26

L et's go to Pahar Ganj," Rohit said later in the
morning, after they had picked up Ramesh's
newspapers and helped him to set up the stall. They
left the station through the main building, where
people were lining up in front of the ticket booths.
One of the three broad fluorescent tubes flickered
from the ceiling, throwing hectic flashes of cold light
over the queues. Swarms of travelers entered and left
through the six wide-open doors. Skinny coolies in
their red jackets haggled with newly arrived tourists
near the taxi stand. Rohit crossed the parking lot,
sure-footed, and Akash had to trot to avoid losing
him in the crowd. When they reached a busy road
Akash stopped to stare at the chaos of vehicles.

Three-wheelers sputtered and cars honked their shrill horns. How would they be able to cross to the other side? But Rohit pulled him by the sleeve. "Come!" He seemed to know which vehicles would stop, and after a quick dash between fenders and front wheels he pulled Akash onto the sidewalk on the other side. Two *peepal* trees stood burdened with banners and advertisements at an intersection, leafless branches entangled in a web of cables. To their right, under a sign labeled PAHAR GANJ MAIN BAZAAR, a street opened, lined with stores on both sides. Cones of white light from the morning sun were reflected in the upper windows. The street was too narrow to allow cars but a tricycle scooter scattered pedestrians out of the way, its horn honking. Ahead, three white men in baggy pants were talking to an old woman. One of the men had long hair, tied in a braid like a girl's. The woman they were talking to held up a tray with rings, smiling at them seductively. Akash practiced more of his English by reading the signs on the buildings along the way. He could make out HOTEL PARADISE in red letters on one roof. A board fastened to the windowsill of a restaurant promised WESTERN FOOD AND EASTERN PRIZES. He wondered what kind of "eastern prize" people would receive in such a place.

Most vendors displayed their wares on tables or piles outside their stores. Suitcases and bags in different colors were stacked against a storefront window. Above the door to a shoe store pairs of sandals were hung on strings like chickens at the butcher's. Armless mannequins wore *salwar kameez* or blouses with tie-dyed patterns that reminded Akash of the fabrics in his village. For a moment he thought of Anu. In his mind he led her along this street, offering to buy her bangles. He would not tell her how he earned the money; he'd just offer her a gift, generously.

Rohit waved at a skinny boy who pushed a cart with shirts and pants spread across the top. "Pradeep, meet my friend Akash!" Rohit pulled Akash closer. Pradeep straightened himself and with a swift movement of his right foot turned the front wheel of his cart so it stopped rolling. "Do you need something?" Circles of sweat grew around Pradeep's armpits from the strain of pushing the cart.

"Yes!" Rohit said. "We need to pick something for Akash."

Akash was not sure what size he should choose. But Pradeep had already unfolded a blue T-shirt and pressed it against Akash's upper body. "Have some pants as well." He shook out a folded pair of dark gray trousers and held them onto Akash's waist. "These are long enough. How many do you want?" Pradeep asked.

Akash looked at Rohit. "We'll take two of each. Just pick different colors." Akash pointed to the dark blue and black ones. Pradeep threw the clothes into a plastic bag and handed it to Akash. No money exchanged hands before they walked on. Akash was just about to ask Rohit about the payment when he saw a small sign announcing MATH TUTOR—ALL STANDARDS—3RD FLOOR.

"Can I meet you back at the platform?" Akash asked. "I would like to go and ask the tutor for his price."

Rohit shrugged. "If you really want to waste money on a teacher, go ahead."

⌊…⌉

Akash followed the arrow under the words and climbed up the three flights of the narrow staircase. A handwritten sign was pinned at the door: DEVENDRA LAL—MATH TUTOR. Akash knocked and when he heard a faint answer he opened the door.

The room was small and dim. The only source of light was a narrow window that opened toward the backyard on the wall facing the door. Half the pane was covered with red cloth. Devendra Lal sat on a blue plastic chair bent over an oval desk in the middle of the room. He was reading a book, his bald head reflecting the pale red light. On the opposite side of the desk stood a second plastic chair, a red one of the same rickety kind that Akash had seen in front of food stalls. The floor was bare except for a dark dhurrie beneath the charpoy next to the door. A tendril of smoke slithered upward from an incense stick on the desk. Akash gave a silent greeting to Saraswati, who played her veena on a poster behind the tutor. This was a good sign. The air was stuffy and the incense burned Akash's eyes, but he forced himself not to sneeze. "*Namaste*, Devendra-ji," he addressed the tutor, his hands folded in front of his chest.

"*Namaste!*" The old man returned his greeting and looked at Akash through thick glasses that made his eyes look huge. "What brings you here, son?"

"I want to study math." Akash now stood behind the backrest of the red plastic chair.

"Do you have money?"

"Yes. How much do you charge?"

"One hundred rupees an hour."

Akash calculated that he could afford about two hours a week if he continued to earn as much money at the train station as he had been. "When can I start?"

"Right now. If you want."

"No. I have to return in two days. Can I come on Monday morning?" Devendra Lal just nodded before he turned his attention back to his book.

27

Akash had spent the morning with Rohit and Sunil jumping in and out of incoming trains, searching the tracks for plastic and paper garbage. When they returned from the recycling station the train from Trivandrum arrived. Trivandrum was a city at the southern tip of India. Akash had seen it on a map in his classroom. "We still need to find a good lunch. Maybe these southerners have left us something," Rohit called, and jumped onto the train as it slowly chugged into the station. They entered the third-class compartment against the stream of weary passengers. Most passengers had very dark skin. The women wore silk saris and their oiled hair gleamed. The three boys scavenged near the entrance of the compartment. Akash hunched down to look at a bag tucked in the corner. "Look at this." He pulled the bag closer. "Someone must have forgotten it."

"Is there food inside?" Rohit called.

"Looks like tiffin containers and something wrapped in banana leaves," Akash answered, as he inspected the contents of the bag.

"Let's take it and get out of here before they notice it and come back," Rohit called. They hurried to the exit and jumped off the train.

"Stop," a policeman yelled as they were making their way through the stream of people. "What are you stealing from the train?"

"Run!" Rohit called, and darted, together with Sunil, toward the staircase. Akash followed, squeezing the bag tightly to his chest.

"Stop!" He could hear the policeman panting behind him.

They zigzagged through the crowds of people. The policeman called out again as they reached the staircase. With a few long strides up the stairs the boys reached the overpass. "Let's squeeze in here," Rohit called. Just as above platform 14, there was a hole in the wire mesh of the fence through which

Rohit now jumped down onto the roof below. Sunil followed. "The policeman won't fit through here. Hurry up!" Rohit called. Akash pushed the food bag through the opening and dropped it into Rohit's open arms. Just before he pushed himself off the edge of the overpass, he turned around and saw the policeman. He was not running anymore, but taking long strides, breathing heavily. Rohit was right. The man would be too fat to fit through the hole.

"Come!" Rohit called. "Now we are safe." The boys walked across the roof toward the end of the platform.

"How do we get off this roof? We can't go back the same way. The policeman might be waiting for us at the hole," Akash said, hoping he wouldn't have to jump down onto the platform from the roof. He couldn't imagine a jump from such a height without getting hurt.

"There is a rope at the end of this roof. We let ourselves slide down and then we meet the others behind the mail sacks," Sunil said.

"You must have run away from the police quite often," Akash said.

"Yes," Rohit said. "But we're almost always faster."

⌊...⌉

When they reached their meeting place behind the mail sacks in the storage building Rohit placed the tiffin boxes on the floor.

"Where are Deepak and Madhup?" Akash asked.

"They would have come if they were hungry," Sunil said, opening the small food containers.

"What's this?" Akash asked looking at the contents of the first tiffin.

"It's *idly*. Here is the *sambar*. They eat this in the south." Sunil held up another container with a yellow soup in it.

The boys divided the contents of the different tiffin boxes equally among themselves and began to eat. Akash thought of the family whose lunch they were eating and hoped that they would have money to buy more food. He tried the white patty Deepak had called *idly*. It had no particular taste. "You have to dip it into the *sambar*. Just like bread," Rohit said, and demonstrated by putting a soaked piece into his mouth. The food tasted different from anything Akash had ever eaten before. "We have to take you to Kerala or Goa," Rohit said. "That's a long train ride, but you see the ocean."

"Guys! It's time to go! We have to hurry."

Deepak suddenly jumped from behind one of the mail sacks, followed by Madhup.

"Where are we going?" Akash asked.

"We have to see Amitabh. He spoke to me just now," Deepak said.

"Amitabh? Amitabh Bachchan?" Akash asked, wondering where Deepak would have seen this most famous of Indian actors.

"Don't be so loud, Deepak," Rohit said. "We don't need anyone to find us here."

"Do you want some food?" Sunil asked.

"No! I'm not hungry!" Deepak yelled.

"Shhhh!" Rohit motioned Deepak to sit down on the floor.

"I will fly away," Deepak said, fluttering his arms. His face distorted to a horrid grin.

"Are they okay?" Akash asked.

"I told you," Rohit said. "The glue makes you see things that are not there."

"At first," Sunil said. "Then it makes you drowsy and when you can't stop it turns your brain into glue."

"But we should go," Rohit said. "It's probably almost one o'clock."

"Where are we going?" Akash asked again, observing Madhup, who was humming as usual, but also swaying back and forth as if drunk.

"To the movies," Rohit answered. "It's Friday. A new film will be released today at Sheila Cinema."

The boys had finished their meal, thrown the empty containers back into the plastic bag, and begun to walk toward the stairs. Deepak moved his arms in a Bollywood dance routine and rotated his hips with each step. Akash stayed behind. Rohit turned around.

"You aren't coming?"

"I don't want to go," Akash said.

"You don't like the movies?" The other boys stared at him in disbelief.

"No." He shrugged. He needed to save the money for the tutor.

Suddenly, he thought of the time back in his village, when his classmate Ravi had started a big cricket game in the schoolyard. The boys had needed one more player, but Akash had said no and sat down in the shade with his notebook. Ravi and the others had gotten angry before they played without him, making a throwaway gesture with their hands on their way back to the field. They thought he just didn't want to join them, but they didn't understand. It was like he was on an island and the others waved at him from the mainland. He *couldn't* be with them.

28

Ramesh was closing the shutters on his stall when Akash returned to the platform.

"Why are you closing so early?" Akash asked.

"It's Navratri today," Ramesh answered. "I'll have to go to the temple."

Akash would have liked to accompany him to the temple, but since Ramesh didn't offer to take him, he didn't dare to ask. Navratri, the nine nights before Dussehra, had always been one of his favorite festivals. In the evenings he had joined the other youths from the village to watch the *dandia* dance. The men would form a circle on the outside and the women one in the inside. When the music began each circle started to rotate slowly in opposite directions. Every time one dancer passed another, they hit their sticks together. Bapu had promised that Akash would get his own *dandia* sticks after his thirteenth birthday. But for one year after Bapu's death no one in his family could participate in any festivals, and he wouldn't have seen the dance this year. Anu too would have to wait to get married until the mourning period was over.

"How come you didn't go to the movies?" Ramesh asked. "Isn't it Friday today?"

"I didn't want to go. I need to save my money for a tutor. I found a man at Pahar Ganj who will teach me math."

"That is very wise of you," Ramesh-ji said, suddenly speaking in English.

"Ramesh-ji, I didn't know you spoke English."

"Maybe you would like to practice your English with me. For the kind of school you want to go to, you need to speak, read, and write English well. Didn't you even bring an English textbook?"

"How do you know English?" Akash asked.

"I used to work as a cook for British people," Ramesh said. "That was a long time ago."

"What was it like? Where did you live?"

"We lived right here in Delhi. They had one of

those old white bungalows. I cooked and cleaned for them. I slept in a little room next to the kitchen. It was a different time."

"Why did you stop?"

"Oh, that is a long story. They left to go back to England and I fell sick. I couldn't get new work for a long time. When a friend asked me to take over this stall, I said yes."

"Why didn't you tell me before that you speak English?" Akash asked.

"I didn't know if you would be worth the effort," Ramesh said. "So many boys just come here and sniff glue and dream of becoming a movie star while their bodies and minds rot away in the train station. But you are different. I've been watching you."

Somehow it didn't sound like an insult when Ramesh told him that he was different. Akash watched as Ramesh walked toward the stairs. Already he was looking forward to the old man's return.

29

Here," Akash said the next evening. "I finished
my exercises." Ramesh had assigned him a
passage in the English textbook. Now Akash pushed
the book toward Ramesh. "I have read the story,
answered the questions, and underlined the words."

"You don't sound very enthusiastic," Ramesh said.

"It's a little boring," Akash said.

"You need to practice *speaking* English," Ramesh
said. "Why don't you take some copies of the *Herald
Tribune* and offer them to those tourists over there."
He pointed to a group of foreigners in Windbreak-
ers, baggy pants, hiking boots, and stuffed backpacks.
"They are probably taking the Shimla Express to get
to the Himalayas and need something to read."

"What do I say to them?" Akash asked in Hindi.

"First of all, you need to address them in English." Ramesh smiled. Akash hadn't even noticed that he had fallen back into his native language. From Mr. Sudhir he had learned a lot of vocabulary, and he could understand well what he read, but to speak the foreign language was still a challenge.

"You smile at them and hold up one of the newspapers and then you ask . . ." Ramesh looked expectantly at Akash.

"You want a newspaper?" The foreign words fell out of his mouth like pieces of spoiled chicken.

"No, you need to be more polite. If you ask this way they will understand you, but it is better to say, 'Would you like to take a newspaper on your long journey?'"

"'Journey'?" Akash didn't know this word.

"'Journey' is another word for trip. *Yatra* in Hindi," Ramesh explained. "Now show me how you will do it."

Akash picked up one of the papers. "Would you like to take a paper on your long journey?" Ramesh nodded. "Very good. Next they will ask how much it costs."

"That is easy. I will say, '160 rupees.'"

"Then they will say, 'That is too expensive.'"

"But that's how much the *Herald Tribune* costs, Ramesh-ji."

"But foreigners like to bargain. You need to make the price a little more expensive when you first mention it so that they feel good when they give you a little less than you have asked."

"Okay, I will ask for two hundred rupees."

"That's better. Now go!"

Akash approached the group of tourists with a few of the English newspapers under his arm.

"Good evening," he began. "Would you like to take an English newspaper on your long journey?"

The three foreigners turned to him, their faces expressing astonishment. What had he done wrong?

"Is that English you're speaking, mate?" asked a burly young man with dark glasses hanging on a string from his neck.

The second man patted him on the shoulder. "This one is cute," he said. Akash felt his face redden.

"You speak English very well," the woman of the group said. She wore her hair cropped shorter than Akash and had a ring pierced through her upper lip. "How much are the papers?"

"220 rupees." Akash was glad that he could say the number without stuttering.

"That's a fair price, I reckon," the burly man said, and pulled his billfold from his back pocket. "Here!" He handed Akash three hundred-rupee bills. "Keep the change."

"Thank you!" Akash said.

Back at the magazine stall Ramesh asked, "How did it go?" He still spoke in English. Akash retold the dialogue and Ramesh laughed when Akash repeated the word "mate." "What does it mean?" he asked.

"That's just a way the Australians address each other. Nothing bad about it," Ramesh said.

"They gave me three hundred." Akash passed the bills to Ramesh.

"That's good," Ramesh said, and pulled a fifty-rupee note out of the cash box. "Here, this is for you. We will do this more often from now on. You get your practice and we both make money."

30

The following Monday morning Akash hurried up the narrow flight of stairs and knocked at Devendra Lal's door. He waited. He knocked again. There was a sound of shuffling inside. "Who's there?"

"I came for the math lesson."

Devendra Lal opened the door carefully and looked at Akash as if he couldn't remember who he was. His light brown kurta looked as if he had slept in it. A yellow stain circled the two top button holes. "You have to pay first," he said as he shuffled back to his chair by the desk. Akash hesitated, but when he saw Saraswati on the poster behind Devendra he remembered what a good omen this was and handed him the money.

"What do you need to learn?"

"I have to prepare for the seventh standard final."

Devendra pulled a sheet of paper from the shelf behind him. When he placed it on the desk the remains of the incense stick rained down on the floor in a fine powder. Next, the old man picked up a pencil from a drawer inside the desk and began to write several lines of equations on the paper. When he finished he turned the paper toward Akash and handed him the pencil. "These are easy," Akash said, and quickly wrote the answers next to the equation sign. He pushed the paper and pencil back to Devendra Lal, who continued with another line of equations. Once again, they did not challenge Akash. "I need to practice simplifying algebraic expressions and factoring," Akash said, after he once again had solved the equations without any effort. "Do you know about factoring?"

"You mean in a multiplication equation such as 2 times 4 equals 8, the numbers 2 and 4 are called factors?"

"No, I mean that 2 and 4 are factors of 8 but when you factor any number you do it like this." Akash was growing impatient. He pulled the sheet of paper toward him and drew the factor tree for 24 on the sheet. "This is an example. You need it when you solve equations with more than one term."

Devendra Lal shook his head. "That's not seventh standard material," he said.

"If you don't know it, then you need to give me the money back." Akash suddenly realized that this man didn't even know as much math as Mr. Sudhir.

"No," Devendra Lal answered. "You bought an hour of my time and the hour has started."

"But you can't help me!"

"That's your problem, not mine. If you want to leave before the time is up, just go!" He shrugged and turned his attention back to the newspaper on his desk. Akash wanted to scream at Devendra Lal for cheating him. But the anger that rose in him was muted by embarrassment that he could have been so easily fooled. He got up and left. In his mind, he blamed himself. He should have asked Devendra Lal some test questions before he even made the appointment. It was his fault that the earnings of more than a day's work were wasted. The loss burned inside Akash as he passed the line of vendors in Pahar Ganj Main Bazaar. How foolish of him to have trusted the sign at Devendra Lal's door that said he was fit to tutor all classes up to twelfth standard.

31

kash didn't want to go straight back to the platform. At the intersection with Pahar Ganj Main Bazaar he turned right and walked farther up the street. The same kinds of stores lined the upper part of the bazaar, some selling clothing, some small trinkets to tourists, some kitchen utensils, but at this early hour the stores were still closed. Some had the shutters down, all doors locked. A street dog hurried past Akash, nervously eyeing him. When he saw two boys, maybe a year or two older than him, turn into a narrow side street, Akash followed them. The boys' hair was neatly cut and their khaki pants had the right length and fit. Both wore dark green vests over white shirts and each carried a leather satchel.

He imagined how they had gotten up in the morning, washed themselves, and put on freshly cleaned and pressed clothes. Akash was sure they lived in real houses with many rooms. Maybe the families even had servants, a maid to clean, a *dhobi* to wash their clothes. Their fathers would have left for work in a car. Their mothers had welcomed them with a good breakfast.

The narrow alley crossed a broad street where traffic was roaring in both directions. The boys turned left and walked a few hundred feet before passing through a metal gate. Akash stopped and backed off when the guard who sat next to the gate caught his eye. A sign on the fence read ST. CHRISTOPHER'S SCHOOL FOR BOYS. Other boys in small groups, all in green vests and white shirts, walked toward the entrance from both sides of the street. Some stepped out of cars, pulling their schoolbags out from the backseat before closing the car door with a loud bang and waving goodbye to the drivers. Suddenly, Akash felt a finger tapping his shoulder. He turned to see a pudgy boy, not much taller than Akash but maybe two years older. He wore thick black-framed glasses. The top button of his shirt was fastened and the tight collar squeezed a ring of flesh out of the starched white fabric. The boy reached down toward Akash's hand, opened his fist, and pressed something into Akash's palm. His fingers were soft and cool.

"Here! Buy yourself some food!"

Akash didn't understand until he saw the ten-rupee note in his hand. He was so surprised that he didn't even say thank you, but just followed the boy with his eyes as he waddled toward the gate.

"What do you think you're doing here?" A deep voice from behind startled Akash. He turned around and the giant hand of a tall Sikh man in a police uniform clasped his shoulder.

"I . . . I . . . I'm just looking," Akash stammered. On the name tag above the man's shirt pocket Akash read SUBIR SINGH.

"Looks like you're doing more than just looking." With his other hand he opened Akash's fist and picked the ten-rupee note from his palm. "Looks like you are begging here!"

"I wasn't begging!" Akash called out, trying to lower his shoulder to get away from the policeman's tight grip.

"That's what they all say!" He turned Akash

around and with a flash of panic Akash saw a police car parked nearby at the curb. "You will come with us to the station. I think we can find a place in a juvenile detention home for a kid like you!"

Akash tried to wiggle himself out of the man's grip. But the policeman was too strong and pushed him toward the car.

"Subir-ji, what are you doing?" Akash heard a woman's voice.

"I found this little beggar outside St. Christopher's and I think we'll bring him in."

"What did he do?" The voice belonged to a female police officer. She now stood next to Akash and looked down on him. She was dressed in the same green-brown uniform as the giant Sikh, but instead of the green turban she wore a canvas hat with the brim flipped up on one side. A gun swung down from her shoulder. Akash had never seen a policewoman. He didn't even know women could work for the police.

"He was begging." The Sikh waved the ten-rupee note.

"I wasn't begging. I just stood there and a boy pressed the money in my hand."

For a moment the two police officers just looked at each other. Then the woman lowered her gaze and looked at Akash. "What's in the bag?" she asked.

"My notebook," Akash said. She took the bag and opened it.

"That's probably stolen from one of the schoolkids," the big Sikh said, shaking Akash.

"Let go of him while we talk," she said. "He won't run while we have his notebook."

"What's a notebook to an urchin like him?" the Sikh said, and Akash could see that he was getting impatient.

She held the notebook in her hand and studied the pages. "What are you doing with a math notebook?"

"I was going to a tutor, but he couldn't help me," Akash said, wondering if the truth would be helpful in this situation.

"Where do you live?"

"At Pahar Ganj," Akash answered. Now the truth would not help.

"Why aren't you at school?"

"I go to the afternoon classes." Akash was thankful that he had come up with another quick lie. The female police officer nodded.

"Why should we believe him?" the Sikh asked.

"He is not dressed like a street kid. Maybe he is telling the truth. And if we take him to the station and his parents complain there will only be trouble." She gave the book back to Akash. What if they asked him for his address?

The policeman's grip was loosening. Akash allowed himself to breathe deeper again. A crackling voice came from the police car. "Calling Officer Singh! Officer Singh?"

"All right. Let's go!" the Sikh finally said. "He's not worth the trouble." The two police officers walked back to the car. Akash saw the tip of the ten-rupee note sticking out from the Sikh's fist. The school bell rang on the other side of the gate.

32

Ramesh had suggested speaking English whenever they were alone at the stall.

"Here, take these." He handed Akash a pile of newspapers written in a language Akash couldn't read.

"What language is this?" Akash asked.

"These are in Gujarati," Ramesh said. "They need to go to a customer of mine who lives in Gurgaon. Once a month I get these from Ahmedabad and I send them to him."

"Should I take the papers to him?"

"No," Ramesh said. "He likes to receive them via mail. He wants the mailman to come to his door."

"You would like me to take them to the post office?"

"Yes! Here is some money." Ramesh had opened the cash box. "They each have to be sent separately."

"Separat— I don't understand."

"Separately, *alag alag*," Ramesh explained in Hindi.

"How much will it cost?"

"There are seventeen papers. They each cost twenty-three rupees to send . . ." Ramesh spoke slowly.

"The total will be 391 rupees," Akash said.

"Oh, you are fast." Ramesh looked at him. "Now here are five hundred rupees."

"I'll bring you 109 rupees in change."

Ramesh shook his head and said, "I guess I won't have to check your math."

"I can show you how to multiply numbers very fast," Akash offered.

"Oh, no!" Ramesh answered. "I won't learn any new tricks. I am fine with my way of calculating. There is no reason for me to be faster."

"Where are the envelopes?" Akash asked.

"Down in the bottom drawer." Ramesh pointed behind the counter.

Akash pulled a pack of envelopes from the drawer

and when he placed them on the counter a photograph fell out.

"Who is this?" Akash studied the black-and-white photograph of a Sikh man with a majestic beard and turban. He was dressed in a dark sports coat, and three medals were hanging from ribbons around his neck.

"That's Balbir Singh Sr., one of India's greatest hockey players," Ramesh said. "The hero of my youth."

"What do you mean?"

"He won a gold medal with the Indian men's Olympic field hockey team in three Olympic Games in a row. In 1956 he carried the flag for India at the Olympic Games in Melbourne."

"How old were you in 1956?"

"I was eleven years old."

"And you loved to play hockey?"

"Yes, that was my dream. I wanted to play for India in the Olympics. But that never happened, of course." Ramesh looked out on the platform with a faraway gaze.

"Did you play good?"

"Did I play *well*?" Ramesh corrected Akash. "For

a while I played all the time, but I was never good enough. My family certainly didn't help me."

"I'm sorry!" Akash remembered that Ramesh had said he knew how it felt to be out of place in one's own family.

"And then I had to work to earn money and the dream burst." Ramesh looked at Akash. "That's why I know how hard it is to hold on to one's dream."

"Could I have *The Statesman*, please?" Neither of them had noticed a customer approaching the stall. Ramesh passed the man the newspaper and took the money.

"English lesson is over," Ramesh said, pushing himself off the stool. "You should go to the post office now and send these papers to my customer."

Akash returned the photograph of Balbir Singh to Ramesh, who looked at the man with the gold medals. Smiling quietly, he put it back into the drawer.

33

The next morning Akash woke up very early and couldn't go back to sleep. He listened to the noises of incoming and departing trains, the jingle that introduced announcements over the loudspeakers, and the voices of travelers and coolies on the platform. He tossed and turned on Bapu's shawl, trying to find a position that was comfortable on the hard concrete roof.

"Why aren't you sleeping?" Rohit asked in a tired voice. "It is too early to be up."

"I'm just thinking."

"What are you thinking?"

"Triangular numbers," Akash said. "They help me to go back to sleep."

"Mmhhh . . . What are those?"

"You get them when you add the previous number to the next, like $1+2=3$, $1+2+3=6$, $1+2+3+4=10$, and so on," Akash explained. "They are a very interesting sequence."

"Stop thinking, start sleeping," Rohit said.

"Do you know why they're called triangular numbers?"

"No." Rohit sighed.

"You can arrange them as a triangle. I can draw it for you," Akash said.

"No, please don't. I'm sleeping."

"Birds often fly in the formation of triangular numbers," Akash said. "I'm sure you have seen it."

"If you are not sleeping, why don't you pick up the papers for Ramesh alone today? I don't want to get up yet. I'll give you my share of the money for it," Rohit said, rolling over on his other side.

⌊. . .⌉

It was just getting light when Akash slipped through the hole in the fence by the slum. The halogen lamp next to the fence threw a cone of light onto the road where Javeed's bicycle rickshaw stood close to the brick wall. The old man was curled up on the backseat, twitching in his sleep like a dreaming dog.

When Akash shook him by the shoulder he let out a deep groan. "Ahhhh, son! Is it time already?"

"Yes, Javeed. Let's go!"

"Ramesh-ji should pay me extra for this night work!" Javeed slowly got up, rearranged his *lungi* around his waist, folded the sheet he had slept under, and tucked it beneath the backseat. "He does, Javeed!" Akash said, and waited for the old man to push the rickshaw onto the road. Akash took his seat in the back and Javeed began to pedal. The truck was already unloading the papers when they reached the corner of Vivekanand Road. Akash grabbed the bundles labeled with Ramesh's name and stacked them onto the rickshaw's backseat before he perched himself on the narrow space left for him to sit.

"You should be pedaling me!" Javeed continued his whining as they slowly rolled back toward the train station. "But youth has no respect for the elders . . ."

Suddenly, a man stepped from behind a wall and jumped in front of the rickshaw. "*Jahaj aa gaya hai,*" the man hissed before he turned around and disappeared in the dark. *The plane has landed.*

"You idiot!" Javeed yelled. "How dare you startle an old man like this!" He had had to step so suddenly on the brakes that his upper body swayed over the handlebars as he tried to regain his balance. "And you have the wrong boy, anyway!"

Akash had tried to make out the man's face, but he had disappeared too quickly.

"What does he mean, 'The plane has landed'?"

"This was a message for your friend Rohit," Javeed said as he began to pedal again. "It's a code for him to go to the pick-up station."

"Which pick-up station?"

"Once a week he goes to Chariband Gali. I have seen him many times coming out of a blue doorway right next to the three-domed mosque after my morning prayer."

"What does he do there?"

Javeed sighed and turned into the street that led to the back entrance of the train station.

"You better ask him yourself," Javeed said. "I don't want trouble with these people."

34

There had been only a twitch in Rohit's eyes when Akash asked him about the man with the message. "Oh, he must have been drunk," he said, dismissing Akash's suspicious look. "I don't know anything about a plane." After they finished unpacking the newspapers Rohit announced that he would go to wash his clothes, but when he left without a bundle Akash quickly followed Rohit from a distance. Traffic was already roaring outside the train station, and for a moment Akash lost sight of Rohit as he crossed the main road to Pahar Ganj. When Akash again saw the red scarf Rohit had entered Chariband Gali, just as Javeed had said. The alley opened to a square where potters displayed dishes and other earthenware on their carts. Akash ducked behind a pyramid of red clay elephants to see where Rohit would go next. Beside the three-dome mosque Rohit walked through a doorway that opened into a short tunnel leading to a courtyard. Akash pressed his back against the wall of the tunnel, following Rohit with his eyes as his friend crossed the courtyard. Three old *havelis* framed the courtyard, each of them with a wooden balcony looming above the cobblestone yard. In a corner, next to a motorcycle, stood a big man dressed in a black leather jacket. Akash watched as Rohit approached him and saw the man reach into the inside pocket of his jacket and pull out a small plastic bag. Rohit took the bag and handed the man a bundle of rupee notes. After this quick exchange, Rohit walked straight back in the direction of the tunnel. Akash ran toward the entrance to leave the tunnel before Rohit saw him, but a three-wheeler blocked the way. The driver honked his horn when he saw Akash approaching. Akash motioned the driver to move backward. But the driver only yelled, honking his horn in a frantic rhythm before he jammed the three-wheeler into reverse gear. Akash's heart beat in his throat as he watched the green-yellow vehicle slowly recede into the square. When he looked back toward the courtyard Rohit was staring at him from the other side of the tunnel.

35

Come!" Rohit yanked on Akash's sleeve, forcing him back out on the square and then motioning Akash up a narrow staircase between two buildings. "Run!" Akash heard Rohit's steps right behind his as he hurried closer to the shaft of light at the top of the stairs. The two boys bent over to catch their breaths as they reached the opening that led to the flat rooftop. The roof was covered with black dust and soot from the nearby ovens. An empty charpoy stood in one corner. Next to it lay a half-eaten chapati, like a waning moon on the dirty cement floor. To one side Akash could see down to the courtyard where Rohit had met the man in the leather jacket. On the other side the roof gave way to a view of the three onion-shaped domes of the mosque.

"What are you doing here?" Rohit asked.

"That's what I want to ask you," Akash answered, looking straight at his friend. "What did you buy from this guy?"

"You shouldn't have followed me," Rohit said.

"Are you dealing drugs?"

"How else can I make the money I need quickly?" Rohit looked at Akash like he had said something dumb.

Two puffed-up pigeons fluttered their wings, trying to push each other away from the flatbread.

"I want to get in," Akash said, surprised by the firm tone in his voice. "I need money quickly too."

Rohit laughed. "You don't play *teen patti*, but now you want to deal drugs?"

"If you can do it, I can do it." Akash kept Rohit's gaze. In his mind he saw himself in the school uniform, wearing a green vest like the boys he had seen at St. Christopher's.

Rohit smiled and shook his head. "I can't believe you, *bhai*! But I could talk to them and see if they will let you in. Are you sure you want to do it? It's dirty work."

"I need about five hundred rupees by next month," Akash answered, thinking about the fees a good tutor would charge. He imagined the principal's smile as she greeted him at the school's gate in the morning before class.

"You must *really* want to get into this school!" Rohit said. "I will put in a good word for you."

The pigeons continued their fight close to the edge of the roof, each of them holding one end of the bread in its beak. One bird spread its wings, trying to lift the bread and fly, but the second pigeon ripped the chapati apart with a sudden jerk, causing both of them to lose the bread. The pieces fell to the courtyard below.

36

They call him the Prince because his father used to be very big in the business," Rohit told Akash on the way to the place the Prince held court. Akash had wondered which business it was exactly and if his father was still alive, but something told him that he wouldn't learn too much about this man. Rohit led the way to a street near Ajmeri Gate. To his surprise Rohit stopped in front of a tea store. A pleasant smell greeted them as they entered. The walls of the store were lined with shelves filled with tin containers and boxes of different sizes, each labeled with a small sign that Akash couldn't read from a distance. Suddenly, a door opened and a giant man motioned the boys toward him. Akash recognized him as the man who had met Rohit in the courtyard. A scar curved from above his right temple down to his cheek. The color and consistency of the man's skin reminded Akash of potatoes.

The back room was sparsely furnished and looked like an office. Two desks faced each other in the middle of the room, with file cabinets adjacent to each. Wooden boxes labeled INDIAN TEA in green letters and adorned with the profile of a woman's face holding a steaming teacup were piled against one wall. Through a small window Akash could see the motorcycle standing in the yard.

A young man with a weight lifter's muscles bulging from the short sleeves of a tight T-shirt sat at one of the two desks. He swung the swivel chair toward the boys and Akash noticed that he wore very tight jeans and black, shiny boots.

"So this is your friend?" The Prince looked at Akash, who averted his eyes to study the large poster of Shiva's head that hung on the wall behind the Prince's chair; the god's skin was tinted blue, with a cobra curled around his neck. "I heard you are good with numbers?" Akash nodded. "I trust that Rohit will show you how the job works. What a shame that we will lose him soon." The Prince shook his head before he focused his eyes back on Akash, who felt like a mouse before a snake. "On delivery day you'll come to the courtyard at Potter's Alley and we will hand you your packages. When your business is finished, we exchange money for more product. Clear?" Akash nodded again.

"Rohit didn't tell me that you were mute. Can you not speak?"

"Yes, I can," Akash said, trying to keep the Prince's gaze.

"Show me your teeth!" Akash looked at Rohit, who nodded encouragingly.

Akash bared his front teeth.

"Step closer!"

The Prince threw a glance at the huge man, who had taken a post at the door.

"Sohan," he called. "Hold his head." Before Akash could move Sohan grabbed his head with both hands from behind and pushed him toward the Prince. The Prince bent forward and pulled Akash's jaws apart before he let his thumb rub over Akash's teeth.

"Nice, strong teeth," the Prince said. Akash gagged, but he couldn't move his head out of Sohan's grip. Slowly the Prince moved his index finger over each of Akash's front teeth. "Don't ever cross me if you want to keep them." The Prince's face was so close to Akash's that he could smell the cardamom and anise on his breath from *paan*. Akash nodded and quickly moistened his teeth with his tongue as the Prince pulled his hand back and Sohan released Akash's head.

"You see this?" The Prince once again came forward in his chair and held his fist under Akash's nose.

Akash nodded.

"This fist will smash your handsome face, break your teeth, and then some!"

Suddenly, the Prince broke into a broad smile. "But my friend with the red bandanna tells me that you are good with numbers and need money urgently. I'm not worried."

Sohan opened the door and light suddenly cut in from the storeroom. The Prince got up. On the back of his upper right arm was a tattoo in the shape of a peacock. The bird's feathers seemed to spread across the man's swollen muscles. In a flash of memory, Akash remembered the Saraswati poster in his old classroom and his teacher's explanation as to why the goddess was shown riding on a swan but with a peacock by her side. When Akash had asked Mr. Sudhir about the peacock, he had answered, "A peacock represents temptations and unpredictable behavior. It reminds us to be careful and wise in following the right path."

37

It was easy. Most time was spent walking from one customer to the next. The actual exchange of money for the drugs was quick. Akash accompanied Rohit on one of his deliveries to Pahar Ganj. Rohit led him through a labyrinth of small alleys and courtyards until they came to a blue door. They both had to lower their heads to enter. It was dark inside and for a moment Akash lost Rohit in the darkness, until his eyes had gotten used to the lack of light. He followed Rohit through a narrow hallway that opened into a courtyard. There Akash recognized Pradeep, the boy who had given Akash T-shirts and pants on his first visit to Pahar Ganj.

Pradeep crouched in the corner, hugging himself, shivering in spite of the warm afternoon weather. "I thought you'd never come!" He sighed. Rohit handed him a small sachet. Pradeep moaned and tried to open it with his trembling hands. Rohit grasped both of Pradeep's hands. "Give me the money now!" Pradeep pulled his right hand out of Rohit's grip and tried to fish something out of the pocket of his jeans. He pulled three hundred-rupee notes out and held them up with two fingers. "Here," he said, turning his attention back to the sachet. Rohit took the notes and held them up like a fan. "Hey, the price is four hundred per bag. You owe me another hundred!"

"I don't have another hundred." He still hadn't opened the sachet.

"No money, no smack!" Rohit snatched the sachet away. Pradeep moaned and let his fingers dive again into his pocket. "All right." He sighed. "Here it is."

[...]

"Now I'm going to introduce you to my best customer," Rohit said. They had entered a street next to Ajmeri Gate and stopped in front of a building with red lanterns hanging from the balcony. Young girls peered through metal grilles, sitting beneath petticoats and skirts hung out to dry. A fat woman in a yellow sari was sitting on a chair in front of a rickety table at the entrance, cracking peanut shells with her short fingers, stuffing the nuts into her mouth, and feeding some to a green parrot in a rusty cage placed in the middle of the table. She looked up and smiled at the boys, flashing two golden front teeth. "Who's your friend?"

"That's Akash. He's going to take over for me."

"You're really going to leave the city to go back to your boring village?" She cracked another peanut and laughed, making the flesh on her upper arms and above the cut of her sari blouse quiver. "Let's go inside. We don't need any eyes on us when we do business."

She led them into a small room next to the staircase. With a sigh she let herself sink onto a small chair behind a desk and pulled out a metal box.

"What do you have?"

Rohit passed her five small bags. She handed him three five-hundred rupee notes. "That's not enough," Rohit said.

"What do you mean?"

"Price is up," Rohit said. "I need a hundred more per bag."

"I don't think so," she said, and suddenly, the jolly expression of her face vanished and her mouth tightened like a clothesline.

"Then I have to take the powder," Rohit said.

"Maybe you want to explain this sudden increase in price to my *pahalvan*?" She gave a sharp whistle and a broad man suddenly filled the doorframe.

Akash looked at Rohit and felt his eyelids flutter, hoping that no one would notice his fear. "It's the Prince who sets the price," Rohit said, not even looking at the bouncer at the door. Akash wondered if it had been a mistake to ask to sell drugs with Rohit. He could never be this tough.

The woman let out an exaggerated sigh, motioned the *pahalvan* to leave, and handed Rohit five hundred-rupee notes.

As they walked back toward the train station Akash asked, "Don't you worry about what will happen if the Prince finds out?"

"Finds out what?"

"That you are charging more than he tells you to."

"He won't find out. He gets his share."

"But someone could tell him."

"The Prince can't be everywhere. Stop worrying!"

Akash, remembering the Prince's threat, let his tongue glide over his teeth.

38

We should split up to save time now. You can deliver this one alone." Rohit handed him another small plastic bag after they left Ajmeri Gate. "We need to leave for the Ram Lila soon."

Akash was looking forward to seeing the final act of the famous Hindu epic that ended the festivities of Dussehra. Rohit and Ramesh had told him that it was staged in front of the Red Fort. He had seen the story of Lord Rama's victory over the evil King Ravana performed in his village, but according to Ramesh it was much bigger in Delhi.

Akash followed Rohit's instructions and turned into the narrow Potter's Alley where arrays of earthen teacups, their openings like rows of tiny gaping mouths, were stacked in front of the pottery ovens. Akash stepped into one of the open sheds. An old potter stood in the corner, stoking the pottery oven with logs. The man's upper body was wrapped in a mud-colored shawl, his skinny legs sticking out from bulging pants pulled up above the knees, giving him a birdlike silhouette. "Rohit sent me," Akash said. "He's in the back," the old man answered, pointing to a rickety doorframe covered with a black plastic sheet. Akash moved the sheet and stepped over the threshold. Dim light fell from the gaps between the wooden boards that made up the walls. A skinny man lay on a charpoy.

"There you are," he greeted Akash, his voice like rolling gravel. The opiate had melted the flesh away from his face and stretched the skin tightly over the bones. Akash recognized the haze in the man's cloudy eyes from Uncle Jagdish's expression after he drank the *bhukki*.

"Where is it?" The man stretched a bony hand toward Akash.

"Give me the money first," Akash said, like Rohit had instructed him to do.

"I have three hundred," the man whispered.

"I need four hundred," Akash said, avoiding the man's eyes.

"I'll give you 350. That's all I have."

"No money, no smack," Akash said, echoing Rohit's words to Pradeep.

"You bastard." The man sighed. He sat up, wrapping himself with his arms. Akash could see that he was trembling. "Bapu!" he called.

The old potter appeared in the doorframe.

"I need a hundred more."

The old man slowly pulled a hundred-rupee bill from his pocket. When he held out his hand to receive the bill, Akash could see all the misery his own family had experienced in the old man's eyes. He quickly looked away.

"Here you go." He threw the sachet onto the charpoy and left the hut.

⌊…⌉

Back on the street, Akash wondered if his Bapu would be watching from the heavens. He could feel his eyes burning on the back of his neck. A searing shame flooded over him. Was this how Saraswati wanted him to follow the path of knowledge? Akash forced himself to multiply today's gain by the number of days in a week. Soon he would have plenty of money to afford a good tutor, someone who could really train his math skills. Akash closed his fist around the bundle of money in his pocket and imagined himself in the white shirt and green vest of the boys at St. Christopher's School.

39

Traffic was already backed up before they even saw the Red Fort in the distance. Cars honked and sputtered black smoke from their mufflers while skinny bicycle-rickshaw-wallahs wildly motioning with their hands tried to wend their way through the stream of vehicles.

"Does Ramesh know how you make money?"

"No," Rohit answered. "And I hope he never does. He doesn't like liars and he especially doesn't like drug dealers. We couldn't stay with him if he knew."

Akash thought about their afternoon English lessons.

"Don't you feel bad about lying to him?"

Rohit shrugged. "He'll never find out."

"What if he does?"

Rohit stopped and shoved Akash lightly. "Could you stop it now? You wanted to sell drugs because you needed the money quickly. Now you have to stop worrying about it. Let's go and have some fun!"

⌊...⌉

The outline of the Red Fort cut against the night sky, its ramparts illuminated by lamps beamed from the ground. A wall of people separated them from the stage and they could only see the top part of the background decorations. To the side stood the large effigies of the evil King Ravana and his son, Meghnath, and brother, Kumbhakarna. The wooden framework of the three demons' bodies was covered with colorful paper in the shape of coats, with short arms sticking out from their firecracker-filled torsos. From a distance Ravana's multiple heads looked like wings attached to his face. At the Ram Lila performances in his village, an idol of Ravana, the evil king of Lanka, had always been burned, but Akash had never seen effigies as large as the ones that towered over the crowd in front of the Red Fort.

"Come!" Rohit pulled his sleeve and entered an alleyway under a banner that read FOOD COURT in bright orange letters. Stalls with snacks lined each side of the narrow path. Music drummed out of speakers so loudly that Akash could feel the hard rhythm of *bhangra* music in his stomach. One stall offered *aloo tikki*. The flat round potato cutlets were neatly placed in the middle of the skillet, their edges sizzling in the hot ghee. The vendor scraped them skillfully into a heap before he turned them over quickly to brown them on the other side. With a swift movement of his hand he rained red pepper powder onto the glistening snack. From afar the sound of religious music pierced the cacophony of rhythms followed by the cackling voice of the narrator.

At the end of the row of vendors, two men quickly shaved thin curls of ice cream from a block into small plastic cups and sprinkled spoonfuls of pomegranate seeds on top before handing them to two young women, whose faces glowed in the light of the neon tube above the sign. Akash couldn't remember the last time he had eaten pomegranate.

"Come on! We can get some on the way back. I'll have money then!"

"But I have money now and I want some!" Akash said, and pulled ten rupees out of his pocket.

The tart taste of the pomegranate seeds merged with the sweetness of the ice cream as Akash squished the juicy pearls between his teeth. He ate slowly, enjoying every spoonful of this sweet delight, before following Rohit through the crowd.

"Aren't we going to the stage?" Akash asked as they were leaving the food court.

"You can go and we'll meet later," Rohit said.

"Where will you go?"

"I'm going over to the parking lot." He winked an eye at Akash. "This is an auspicious day to win some money."

Akash remembered their trip to Agra. How naïve he had been then, thinking Rohit made money from selling plastic bottles and helping Ramesh.

"How will I find you in this chaos?"

"You can come with me first, so you know where I'll be."

He followed Rohit until they reached the first row of cars parked on the field to the side of the food court. He could still see the three effigies standing. They wouldn't be set on fire until the very end of the play, when Lord Rama had freed Sita and, with the help of Hanuman, defeated Ravana and his son and brother.

Rohit walked toward a group of men sitting on the pavement next to their cars.

"How do you know these men?" Akash asked.

"I don't know them. I just know their game. They hang out here until the show is over and then they bring their rich masters back home. In the meantime they are bored, so they like to play cards," Rohit said.

"You came here to play cards, not to see the Ram Lila?" Akash was disappointed.

"You should go as close to the stage as you can and we can meet here at this corner when it is over."

Rohit was already focused on the men and following their game. After they finished their hand, one of them looked up at Rohit and asked him to join.

"Do you play?" a man in a purple shirt asked Akash. Akash shook his head and buried his hands deep in his pockets.

"Yes, he plays!" Rohit called. "He just learned the game!" Akash wanted to protest, but the men had already made a space for him on the pavement to join their game. Two cards flew into the empty space, beckoning Akash to try his luck. Each of the men threw a twenty-rupee bill in the middle before they took more cards.

Maybe it was the rush of sugar in his blood or

the feeling of the wad of money in his pocket that caused a lightness he hadn't felt in a long time. Suddenly, the dark memories of Uncle Jagdish didn't hold him back anymore. Akash picked up the cards and joined the group of men, sitting on his haunches. His first game was cautious. He hadn't thrown too much money in the middle, but he won. Due to a bad starting hand in the second game, he knew not to bet too much, and he lost. For the third game he was dealt two aces. He threw a fifty-rupee note into the middle and focused on the other players. The man in the purple shirt apparently also thought he had a good hand. He continued to up the money until they both had to show their cards. But Akash won, and when the man brushed the bills toward Akash his cheeks were pleasantly flushed.

Suddenly, a shot exploded in the air. "They're starting."

Rohit had already gotten up and motioned Akash to follow.

"Let's look at the burning of Ravana." Since the crowd was too dense to allow them a good view, Rohit turned toward the public toilet on the corner of the parking lot. Several men had already climbed onto its roof. Quick as a monkey Rohit used the windowsill to reach the top and bent down to pull Akash up. From their rooftop porch they could see the fire ravaging the effigies of the evil king and his son and brother. Burning scraps of paper flittered in the air as the papier-mâché effigies caught fire and quickly burned from the bottom to the top. The crowd cheered and Akash roared with the thousands on the square.

⌊...⌉

"That was fun," Akash said to Rohit as they climbed through the hole in the fence to return to the platform. He still felt the warm glow of winning.

"You see," Rohit said. "It feels great to make money!"

Akash nodded, then he froze. Sohan in his black leather jacket was standing on the overpass, right next to the stairs leading down to their platform.

"The Prince wants to see you," he said.

Rohit stuttered, "But . . ."

"Now!" Sohan said, and pushed them both toward the exit.

40

Sohan had parked the car on Asaf Ali Road. At this time of night the shutters of most stores were closed and only a few windows were open and lit. They walked silently past a few storefronts before Sohan turned into a dark alley. Akash recognized from their previous visit the dirty billboard advertising *paan* under a dim neon light at the corner. They were walking toward the back entrance of the tea store, and there stood the Prince waiting for them outside. He leaned against the wall and when he saw them coming he flipped the stub of his cigarette into the street. Akash wondered if the others could hear the loud drumming of his heart. He glanced over at Rohit, who just stared ahead.

"Did you think I was stupid?" The Prince spoke quietly. Sohan grabbed the back of Rohit's neck and pushed him toward the Prince. "I can't hear you, pretty boy!"

Sohan shook Rohit and Akash felt the shake as if Sohan's fist were grabbing him.

"I didn't think you were stupid," Rohit finally said.

"Then why did you skim money off me?"

"I am sorry!" Rohit said.

"I am sorry too. This ruins my business. I decide the prices for my dope. If you change the price my customers might prefer the competition. That's bad for business!"

Sohan suddenly grabbed Rohit from behind with both hands and lifted him off the ground.

"Do you have any money on you?" The Prince sifted through both of Rohit's pockets and pulled out the rupee bills he had won at the card game. "This is mine!"

The Prince swung his fist into Rohit's face. Rohit's head fell to one side and he released a loud sigh of pain.

"I didn't mean to," he stammered.

"But you did! You'll pay me back!"

Akash could only stare at his friend, who hung in Sohan's grip like a doll.

"Did you know about this?" The Prince's dark eyes now focused on Akash.

"He had nothing to do with it!" Rohit whispered.

"He had nothing to do with it?" The Prince stepped closer to Akash.

Frozen like a rat in front of a snake Akash stared at the Prince, awaiting a punch. But suddenly Sohan screamed, "The bastard bit me!" He dropped Rohit, who quickly scrambled back to his feet. But as he ducked to escape, the Prince grabbed him by the shoulder. "You stay here!" he yelled. With his other arm he pulled Akash closer.

"Listen to me!" He shook both boys and waited until they turned their eyes toward him. "You will pay your debt! I'll give you two days. If you don't leave two thousand rupees in the tea store by next Wednesday, I'll come and get you. And we know where to find you." With a shove he let go of Akash and Rohit. The Prince straightened himself, pulling his pants up by the belt loops. "I am done working with kids. You will never get back into this business!"

The Prince motioned to Sohan and the two

disappeared into the darkness. Akash looked at Rohit. A thin red line was running like a crack in an earthen vessel down the side of Rohit's face. Rohit just nodded and wiped his temple with the back of his hand, leaving a red smudge.

41

They didn't talk for a long time. There was only the sound of their slapping sandals on the sidewalk. Akash's thoughts were darting around like mice in a cage. He still saw the Prince's face and his warning echoed in his ears. Now they would lose all their money. If they shared the debt equally Akash would have only five hundred rupees left. That was barely enough to pay for one or two lessons with a better tutor.

They passed a row of bicycle rickshaws parked against the curb. On each rickshaw a driver lay sleeping, skinny human bundles wrapped in threadbare shawls, their creased soles sticking out to the side.

They crossed another intersection, but at this time of night there was no traffic, only their shadows rushing across the dark storefront windows as they neared the train station.

Akash couldn't bear the silence anymore. "What are we going to do now?"

"I'll take the train to Ajmer," Rohit answered.

"You don't want to give the Prince the money back?"

"I can't. I need the money for my mother."

"But I can't leave," Akash said.

"Why not?" Rohit stopped and looked at him. "Take a train to Mumbai or Calcutta. Now you know how to survive in a train station. And they teach math anywhere."

They walked on and Akash considered a train to Mumbai or Calcutta. But he didn't want to leave Ramesh, the first good person who had taken an interest in him after Bapu's death.

Back on the roof of Ramesh's stall, Rohit sat down on the cement and pulled a wrapped bundle from under his sheet.

"Don't look at me like a beaten dog," Rohit said. "I always told you I would leave. Diwali is coming up. I promised my mother that I would be back by then. I'm not going to lose all the money now."

"But if I want to stay *I* have to pay the debt. You should give me at least half of it. It's not my debt alone." Akash sat down across from Rohit.

Rohit looked at Akash. His eyes were suddenly hard.

"Why don't you get out of Delhi?"

"I don't want to leave Ramesh," Akash said.

Rohit shook his head. "There will be another magazine-wallah in another train station."

"Give me at least a thousand rupees," Akash demanded.

"No." Rohit had finished packing and slung his bag across his shoulder. "The Ajmer train leaves in half an hour. You should go on the Mumbai Express. It leaves from platform 3 in the morning."

Akash had pulled out his savings. He counted 1,500 rupees. "If I pay the Prince to leave me alone," he said. "I need another five hundred rupees."

Rohit pulled out five hundred-rupee bills and threw them into Akash's lap. "Here," he said. "That's all I'll give you." He got up. "You're making a stupid decision. I thought you *really* wanted to go to a good school. That won't happen here if you can't make money from drugs."

Rohit reached the ladder and began climbing down.

"Ramesh is not worth losing all your savings!" he said before his face disappeared.

Akash watched Rohit as he walked away. Then he added the five hundred rupees to his bundle, fastened it with a rubber band, and wrapped the money in Rohit's sheet. He would sleep for a few hours until it was time to pick up Ramesh's newspapers. On the way he would leave the money at the tea store.

42

After he had dropped off the money Akash was in no hurry to return to the platform. He walked aimlessly, thinking about the money he had just lost and how his goal seemed to have disappeared again into the far distance. When he passed the wall surrounding a small park, Akash entered through a low gate, following a palm-lined gravel path leading toward a fountain. Not many people were walking on the maze of trails. Only a few guards stood listlessly with their sticks, and Akash eyed them, making sure he would not attract their suspicion. Parrots flew screeching from tree to tree, chasing other birds off the branches. To the left side of the path someone had planted a plot of marigolds. The gardener must have had a sense for geometry, since the plants were arranged in four smaller rectangles divided by low hedges. Akash stepped closer to the fence and counted eleven rows with twelve plants in each quadrant. That meant 132 plants in each small rectangle; multiplied by 4 they equaled 528. In his mind Akash added the digits and envisioned the result, 15, as a tree of factors . . .

He stopped himself.

These numbers that rolled around in his head as easily as marbles had brought only pain. His teacher, Mr. Sudhir, had called it a gift; others had envied his talent. They didn't know what it had made him do. Saraswati had abandoned him. Ganesha had refused to remove the obstacles. Akash picked up a handful of gravel and threw it at the sunny blossoms. He didn't want his mind to play with numbers anymore, but how could he stop doing what came as naturally as breathing?

"You don't like marigolds?" The voice startled Akash. He looked around and saw a sadhu, a holy man, sitting under a tree. The sadhu, dressed in a saffron robe and pants and a turban of the same shade, motioned Akash to come closer. His trident, a three-pronged fork on a wooden stick, was leaning against the tree.

"I do like marigolds," Akash mumbled, feeling embarrassed that someone had seen his outburst.

"Come over here," the sadhu called.

Akash had heard stories about the magical powers of these wandering holy men who had turned their backs on all worldly pursuits in hope of achieving *moksha*, liberation from suffering, through the contemplation of the gods. They would occasionally pass through his village on their journeys from one sacred place to the next. These men had the power to bless weddings and newborns but were also known to cast spells on people. Akash didn't want to offend a sadhu and for fear of attracting the man's evil eye he reluctantly stepped closer.

"Why so troubled, young man?"

"I'm not troubled," Akash said.

"Trouble hangs on you like a bad smell." The man's dark face was circled by a furry frame of white hair like that of a langur monkey. His piercing black eyes looked knowingly at Akash.

Akash stared down at his feet. He didn't want to talk about his troubles.

"Why don't you stay with me for a while and tell me your story?" the sadhu said, filling his chillum pipe with dried leaves he pulled from a satchel. He nodded at Akash before lighting his pipe and soon a sweet smell wafted from his nostrils.

"There is no story to tell," Akash said.

The sadhu stretched out under the tree. "You are too young to feel the pain of love but you have felt the pain of loss. Most other pain comes from longing for something that is not ready to come to you. The gods don't like to be hurried."

Akash felt a warm blush coloring his cheeks. This sadhu could read his mind.

"Oh, the pain of wanting," the sadhu said, exhaling another cloud of sweet smoke. "You are trying to reach the top of the mountain, but you don't want to climb. Only a bird can get there without climbing."

Akash turned to leave. He didn't want to hear any more.

On his way back toward the street Akash heard the sadhu giggle and call after him, "You have no wings, young friend."

43

The gods don't like to be hurried. *The gods don't like to be hurried.* The sadhu's words echoed in Akash's head as he walked back toward the train station. *The gods don't like to be hurried.* The old sadhu was right. Saraswati did not help him because Akash had tried to force her. Akash had just wanted to show the gods that he was worthy of their support. That he *really* deserved to be granted his wish. But Saraswati would decide when it was time.

Akash slowly took the steps down to the platform, keeping close to the banister, away from the stream of passengers. In the distance he saw Ramesh taking magazines from a box and placing them on the counter.

"There you are," Ramesh said. "I was wondering what had happened to you boys this morning."

"Rohit left. He went back to his village to buy medication for his mother."

"That was quick. I wonder why he didn't say goodbye." Ramesh looked out at the platform and then back at Akash. "You look sad. Do you miss him already?"

"No," Akash said. "I knew he would leave. Now I can take over his shift." He tried to smile, but his face felt stiff.

"I might have a solution for your money problem. My friend Yogesh will soon need a full-time helper." Ramesh arranged the pile of magazines he had pulled out of the box.

"Who is Yogesh?"

"He has a juice stall on platform 1. His boy has disappeared and right now he is working without help." Ramesh laughed. "He thinks all boys are unreliable. But I know that soon he will want to have a new helper. Wouldn't this be something for you?"

"How much does he pay?" Akash asked.

"Fifty rupees per day, and he gives you food. Together with what you earn here you could save money for a tutor."

Akash nodded and forced himself not to calculate when he would have earned enough to pay for a tutor. It would take a long time, but he would earn the money with honest work. *You have no wings, young friend.* He heard the sadhu's words again.

Ramesh had climbed on top of his stool, but as he stretched to open the topmost clothespin the stool began to sway and fell to the side. Ramesh tried to regain his balance by holding on to the line, but it ripped and he plunged down. Akash rushed toward the stall to help.

"Are you all right?" Akash called. Ramesh was lying on his back on the floor.

"My shoulder," the old man cried.

"Can you get up?" Akash asked, and bent down, offering his hand.

"I don't know." Ramesh tried to lift his right arm, but collapsed with a sigh of pain. "I can't move my right arm. It struck the counter during my plunge," he said.

"Try to give me your left arm and I'll pull you up carefully." Akash helped the old man up and steadied the stool for him to sit.

"That darn stool," the man said as he sat down, holding his right shoulder with his left hand.

"You need to see a doctor!" Akash said.

"I need to lock up my stall before I go." Ramesh opened a drawer under the counter, but the movement brought a new sigh of pain. He passed Akash the key. "You need to pull down the shutter, after you have cleared the counter. Just push everything onto this side."

After Akash had closed the bookstall according to Ramesh's instructions he asked, "Can you walk to get a three-wheeler?"

Ramesh nodded. "The government hospital is not far."

"Then let's go," Akash said.

⌊···⌉

The emergency room smelled like stale curry and sour sweat. A crowd of people stood around a desk in the middle of the room, screaming and yelling at one another, fighting for the attention of a slim man behind a sign that read DR. MALHOTRA—CASUALTY MEDICAL OFFICER ON DUTY. The doctor issued orders to a nurse, who picked a woman with a bleeding child in her arms out of the crowd. Akash looked around to find a place for Ramesh to sit, but all chairs were taken, so he led Ramesh to a corner of the room where he could sit on the floor while Akash went to find help. Akash tried to squeeze his way through the crowd to the doctor's desk, but two men with bright red turbans pushed him back. The taller of the two pointed to the other side of the room, where an older man who wore the same kind of turban had collapsed on a chair, his right eye bandaged. "Our father was here first." Akash stepped back from the crowd and looked around. He suddenly realized that in his pocket he still had three hundred rupees he had won at the Ram Lila card game. Maybe he could bribe someone to take a look at Ramesh.

A second doctor entered the room, and before he could take a seat behind the desk Akash blocked his way. "Please take a look at my uncle, doctor-ji. I think he broke his arm."

"Where is he?" the doctor asked. Other patients were calling for the new doctor and before he could turn his attention elsewhere Akash pulled him by the sleeve.

"Over there." The doctor followed him to the corner. No bribe was necessary.

"What happened?" The doctor bent down in front of Ramesh.

"I fell off a chair and hit the stone counter of my store. Now I can't move my right arm."

"Your uncle needs to have an X-ray taken." The doctor pulled a pad from the pocket of his white coat, scribbled instructions, and handed Akash the slip of paper.

"The ward boys are all busy, so you should take him to the X-ray room yourself. It's down the hall."

44

Ramesh was holding on to a young female doctor's arm as he staggered out of the X-ray room. "How is he?" Akash jumped up from the chair in front of the door.

"I have given him an injection against the pain and he is very drowsy," the doctor answered as she led Ramesh to a chair in her office. She attached the X-rays to a white box and turned on a light switch that illuminated the picture from behind.

"This fracture cannot be healed with a cast alone," the doctor said as she studied the black-and-white shadows on the picture.

Ramesh had closed his eyes and seemed to have fallen asleep.

"Is this his bone?" Akash asked, pointing to a white oblong shape.

"Yes," the doctor said. "And you see how it is splintered up here." She indicated an area on the top part of the X-ray with the back of her pen.

"What does it mean that it can't be fixed with a cast?" Akash asked.

"It means that we will have to operate and screw a plate into the bone."

"A plate?" Akash asked.

"Yes. We will use a small metal plate to connect the two larger pieces of the bone so that he can move his arm again." The doctor turned and looked at Akash.

"How much does it cost?" Akash asked.

"This is a government hospital. So the operation and medication are free. But you will have to pay for the plate and the screws."

"How much?"

"Between two and three thousand rupees."

"And you won't operate until he pays?"

The doctor bobbed her head quickly. "Naturally. The hospital needs at least a 10 percent down payment."

"How long can he stay like this?" Akash pointed to Ramesh.

"It's best to operate right away. That will guarantee that his arm functions properly again. I have an empty spot in one hour since we canceled a scheduled procedure. If you have the money for a down payment, we could fix his arm today."

Akash nodded. "Yes," he said. "I can pay right now." He pulled out his three hundred rupees.

The doctor sat down at her desk and filled out a form. "Take this paper to the cashier and pay the bill. They will tell you how to get to the nurses' station from there."

Akash took the form and gently woke up Ramesh. "We need to bring you to the nurses' station. Let's walk."

"What are they going to do now?" Ramesh asked, his voice slurred from the painkiller.

"They will have to operate on your shoulder." Akash offered his arm and Ramesh got up. He slowly led Ramesh down the corridor until they found an empty chair. "Why don't you sit here and wait while I take care of the paperwork?"

"But they will ask for money," Ramesh said.

"No need to worry about money right now," Akash said. "I'll take care of that."

A long line queued in front of the cashier's counter. As he slowly moved ahead in line Akash thought about how good he felt using the money to help Ramesh. He had no doubt. This was the right thing to do.

45

Ramesh was sitting upright in his bed, his arm and shoulder bandaged. The tall doctor who had performed the operation stood next to the bed.

"There you are." She turned to Akash.

"*Namaste.*" Akash folded his hands and bowed to greet her before he turned to Ramesh.

"How are you, Ramesh-ji?"

"Better," he said. "This nice lady doctor fixed my arm without delay."

"Yes," she said. "Thanks to your nephew here who put money down for the plate in your arm and filled out all the forms, we could perform the operation right away. That was good since the splinters could have injured your nerves. Now you only have to keep the cast on for a month and your arm will be just like before."

"When can he go home?" Akash asked.

"Will you take care of him?"

"Yes," Akash said. "I will take care of him and his magazine stall."

"Akash stays with me in my small flat," Ramesh said, winking at Akash. "It's not big but enough for the two of us."

"I'll have to leave you now to attend to my other patients. Goodbye." The doctor turned toward the man in the next bed.

"I can stay with you in your flat?" Akash asked.

"I think you shouldn't sleep on top of my stall anymore. Would you like to live with me?"

Akash nodded.

"Look at that smile on your face." Ramesh chuckled and reached out with his good arm to squeeze Akash's shoulder. "Now I am going to give you my key and I'd like you to go to my flat right away and get money to pay for the rest of my bill so I can go home."

Only one booth was open at the cashier's, and the woman behind the glass had put out a sign asking customers to "pull a number." Akash ripped the number 89 from the roll while the digital screen next to the cashier's window changed with a low buzz to 17. There were no seats inside the cashier's office and Akash went back out into the hallway, where he had seen an empty bench. He would have to wait a long time until it was his turn, since seventy-two people had pulled numbers smaller than his. One seat on the wooden bench was now occupied by a boy. As he sat down Akash recognized the green vest with the words ST. CHRISTOPHER'S embroidered in white cursive. It was the same boy who had pressed the ten-rupee note into Akash's hand in front of St. Christopher's School. The boy was holding a booklet. Akash peeked over and saw that he was solving a number puzzle made from a grid of nine squares, each containing three-by-three smaller boxes partially filled with one-digit numbers. The boy was filling the empty squares according to a pattern. Akash strained his eyes trying to figure out the rule the boy followed as he distributed the numbers. Akash noticed that each individual box within one of the nine larger squares contained the numbers one through nine only once. But how did the boy decide where to place them? When he had finished the top three of the nine larger squares Akash saw that the digits from one to nine also appeared only once in each longer row. The rule to solve the puzzle must be to distribute the numbers so that in each row and column and in the smaller three-by-three squares, the numbers from one through nine only appear once.

"Why are you staring at me?" The boy looked up and turned to Akash. His thick glasses made his eyes seem large.

"I'm just looking at your puzzle," Akash said. The boy did not recognize him.

"It's called sudoku. It's a Japanese word meaning 'one single number,'" the boy said.

"Do they teach you Japanese at St. Christopher's School?"

"No." The boy shook his head. "I just know this because it says so in the front of this booklet." He showed Akash the inside cover page.

"Is this entire booklet filled with these puzzles?" Akash asked.

"Yes." The boy nodded. "Would you like to try solving one?"

"Sure," Akash said, and the boy ripped the next page off the brochure and handed Akash a pen from his pocket. "There is one on the front and one on the back of the page. Do you know the rules?"

"You have to fill all rows and columns as well as the smaller three-by-three squares with the numbers one through nine," Akash said.

"That's right," the boy said. "This is just the easy version. The booklets come with easy, medium, and difficult sudokus."

Akash had already begun to solve the puzzle. It was not very hard and the empty squares filled quickly.

"Hey," the boy said. "You're good at this."

"Thank you," Akash answered. "I like numbers."

"Me too," the boy said. "But I'm not as fast as you are."

"You need to scan the rows for the numbers that are already there. Here for example you start with the ones. Then you draw a line through the columns and rows that already contain a one. This way you eliminate all the fields where a one cannot be placed and are left with the fields where a one can be put."

"Wow, you figured this out in no time. It took me forever to learn these little tricks," said the boy.

"What kind of math do you practice in school?"

"I'm in seventh standard. We do some geometry and fractions and decimals. The sudokus I solve just for fun."

"What's your name?" Akash asked.

"I'm Manish."

"I'm Akash. Are you also waiting to pay a bill?"

"No, I'm waiting for my mother. She works here and I am supposed to pick her up. But she's often late."

"I'm waiting to pay the bill for my uncle. He broke his arm."

"Is it bad?"

"No," Akash said. "We were lucky and had a very nice doctor who operated on him right away. Now he just has to keep his cast on but can go home."

"There is my mother," Manish said.

"I'm sorry I am late," the woman said. It was the doctor who had operated on Ramesh.

"Mama, meet Akash."

"We have already met. He helped his uncle to get the operation right away," she said, smiling.

"But you fixed his arm. Thank you, again," Akash said.

"Akash is a sudoku master," Manish said. "And he hadn't ever solved any sudokus before today. I gave him one and he solved it super fast. He is a natural."

"I'm not surprised after what your uncle has told me about you," the doctor said.

Akash looked down. This was not a good time to remind him of his dream.

"Ramesh-ji also told me that you have very ambitious plans," she continued. "Manish goes to the St. Christopher School and I know the principal very well. I could call her and ask her to give you an appointment. If you really are as good as Ramesh says, you might have a chance to be admitted with a scholarship."

"Yes," Manish said. "That would be great. Then we could solve sudoku puzzles during break. Not many other boys like numbers more than cricket."

"There is no guarantee that it'll work, but at least you would have a chance to talk to the principal of a very good school," the doctor said.

"Thank you," Akash said. "That would be wonderful." He could feel his face stretching into a broad smile.

"Let's go now!" the doctor said.

"Nice meeting you!" Manish said. "I'll make sure she calls the principal soon. I could use a friend at St. Christopher's."

Akash hurried back to the cashier's room to see if his number had come up yet before sharing the good news with Ramesh.

46

Before they left Akash had to show Ramesh his fingernails. Ramesh also inspected his ears. "They will not look into my ears," Akash protested, but Ramesh turned Akash's head and pulled his left earlobe without comment. Akash knew he had to wear his best shirt and clean, pressed pants. As they prepared to leave, Ramesh pulled out a pair of shoes. "Put these on," he said. "I can go in my slippers, but you need to have real shoes."

Akash examined the shoes. They were just like the kind worn by the boys who went to St. Christopher's.

"They'll be a little big," Ramesh said. "But they'll work. Here is a pair of socks too."

Akash sat down to put on the shoes.

"'Shoes make the man.' That's what Mr. Haddock, the British gentleman I worked for, used to say." Ramesh knelt down on one knee and dusted the leather against his sleeve with his good arm. Akash's feet felt stiff in the shoes and he had to walk slowly at first.

"Make sure you don't stumble when we get there," Ramesh warned. "Don't make it look like this is your first time in shoes."

⌊…⌉

At the gatehouse to the school, Ramesh signed his name in a thick ledger. "This is my nephew," he said to the man in the blue uniform behind the window. "We're here to see the principal." With a buzz the heavy steel gate jumped from its lock and Akash helped Ramesh to push it open.

Mrs. Sharma, the principal, was a tall, angular woman. She greeted them in the hallway in front of her office after only a short wait. With her sinewy long neck, black hair symmetrically parted, and collarbones protruding sharply, she seemed to consist mainly of straight lines. She wore a dark green sari made from stiff silk, the gold border running a perfect diagonal across her flat chest. They followed her into her office and Akash could smell the jasmine blossoms that hung on a thin string from the tight bun of her hair. She asked Akash and Ramesh to be seated in the two chairs. Mrs. Sharma sat upright behind her desk on a chair that seemed higher than those of her visitors. After she had rested her folded hands on the desk she asked, "What brings you here?"

"This is my nephew, Akash," said Ramesh. "He has a gift for numbers and he would like to be accepted in your school."

"I understand that you told my secretary that you have no documents or any papers." Akash noticed that her hands were soft and delicate.

"No, we lost everything in the fire in our village."

They hadn't talked about how they would explain their lack of any school documents, and Akash was surprised at how easily Ramesh came up with a story. He wanted to smile at him but knew not to.

"We cannot enroll anyone without previous assessment of their academic aptitude." Akash wasn't sure what the word "aptitude" meant, but from the frown on Mrs. Sharma's forehead he could tell that it was very important. Akash averted his eyes as she focused her stern look on him. He needed her to like him, but he couldn't hold that stern gaze of hers.

"You could give him a test," Ramesh said. He seemed unperturbed by her intimidating appearance and stared right at her.

"The only test he could take would be the final exam of the class previous to the one he would want to attend next year," Mrs. Sharma answered. "Where is he currently attending school?"

Akash looked at Ramesh. He wished now that they had rehearsed the interview and thought of the possible questions she could ask.

"Akash is not enrolled in any school. He just arrived in Delhi and we chose your school," Ramesh answered.

"Even if he were to be accepted on the basis of his academic performance"—Mrs. Sharma paused for a moment, adjusting herself on the chair—"would you have the means to support a child at our school?"

"I was hoping Akash would qualify for a scholarship," Ramesh said.

"So you are quite confident in your nephew's abilities?" Mrs. Sharma asked.

Ramesh nodded. "Yes, I am."

"Obviously, I cannot make any promises. He would have to do very well in order to receive a scholarship. Even our best students seek out the help of tutors."

She swallowed and the small hollow between her collarbones jumped.

"Do you recommend tutors?" Akash asked.

"Yes, we have a list." She opened a drawer and passed him a sheet of paper. "But they are not cheap."

"Could I take the exam needed to enter next year's class?"

Mrs. Sharma looked at him. He forced himself to hold her gaze. *Please help me*, he thought. Suddenly, she relaxed slightly and unfolded her hands. She leaned against the backrest of her chair—and smiled.

"You really want to go to this school, young man," she said, her voice softer.

Akash nodded. He needed to swallow before he could answer. "Yes, I really want to go to your school. Ramesh, I mean, my uncle, and I will find the money for the tutors."

Ramesh nodded slowly. "My nephew has a job and he lives with me," he said, and looked at Akash encouragingly.

Mrs. Sharma took a deep breath and leaned forward. Her delicate hands were now spread flat on the desk's surface.

"I can sign your registration for the March exam. You'll have five months to prepare." Mrs. Sharma took another sheet of paper from her drawer. "What is your full name?"

47

The next day back at the train station Akash walked over to platform 3 and watched the man at the juice stand from afar. Yogesh was thin and tall, a few years younger than Ramesh. He stood behind a table with a fruit press. Empty rinds of limes and oranges lay scattered around on a red tablecloth. Akash watched Yogesh work for a while. He saw him press the fruit and hand glasses of juice to customers in exchange for money. Yogesh smiled at his customers and Akash could hear him speak in English when he sold juice to foreigners.

When he caught Akash's eye Yogesh called out to him. "What are you looking at, boy?"

Akash walked over to the juice stand and introduced himself. "I work for Ramesh, but I need another job."

"Oh, you want to have two jobs?"

"Yes. I need money to prepare for school and good tutors are expensive," Akash said. "But I can only work half days since I need time to study and I also want to help Ramesh."

"Ramesh mentioned your name and if he recommends you, I am willing to give it a try," Yogesh said. "The hours are no problem. I'll pay you fifty rupees a day. You can start right now, if you want to."

Akash nodded and they shook hands.

"You learn fast," Yogesh said, after he had shown Akash how to use the press to squeeze the oranges and limes. When Yogesh left for a moment an old woman in a thin sari came and asked for a fresh lime soda. Akash squeezed the lime juice into one of the thick glasses he had just dried and opened the cap of a soda bottle. When he poured the water into the glass, the liquid fizzed. "Would you like sugar or salt with it?" Akash asked. The woman pointed to the sugar pot and Akash added a spoonful of the white crystals, causing the water to hiss again. Then he passed the glass to the woman. She gave him a ten-rupee bill. As he pulled out the box with change from under the desk the woman said, "No, no! Keep the change!"

Akash said, "Thank you!" and let the bill fall into the box.

Suddenly, Yogesh touched Akash's shoulder.

"You startled me!" Akash cried.

"Sorry, but I just wanted to see if you were honest. So I stood behind you while you served the woman. I'm glad that you put the bill back into the box. Many of the boys I've tried didn't. It looks like we're going to get along well together."

Around noon, after Yogesh had asked Akash to tend to the stall while he went to his temple, Sunil, Deepak, and Madhup came down the stairs to platform 3.

"We thought you had left us," Sunil said. "Where have you been?" Akash told them about Ramesh's accident and Rohit's departure to his village.

"I knew Rohit would go back to his village," Sunil said.

"He must have had enough money," Madhup mumbled.

"What are you doing now at Yogesh's juice stall? Did you give up working for Ramesh?" Deepak asked.

"No, I need more money for school, so I took on a second job," Akash said.

"School?" Deepak asked. "Now that's a waste of money!" He shook his head.

"Hey," Sunil said. "Speaking of money, we can share what's in this cash box." He bent over the counter, but Akash pushed him back.

"No," he said. "You won't take any of Yogesh's money."

"Hey, hey, hey." Deepak jumped back and turned in one of his spinning dance moves. "You are no fun!"

"He never was," said Sunil, and Madhup just bobbed his head. "Let's go!"

Akash watched the boys disappear in the crowd on the platform. He wouldn't miss them. He picked up the knife and cut another orange in half, looking out for the next customer. This was a good place to work.

In the evening, when they had closed the newsstand, Ramesh asked Akash to come home with him. On their way Ramesh pointed to a sweets stall.

"Let's buy some *ladoos* and bring them to the temple. I think we both have reason to be thankful."

"Yes," Akash said. "I would like to thank Saraswati."

"And Ganesha has removed obstacles for both of us," Ramesh continued. They each bought a small package of sweets to take as offerings to the gods. As they continued on they passed a group of boys, dressed in the uniform of a private school, each with a book bag dangling from his shoulder. Akash remembered how he had previously felt when he saw neatly dressed children in polished shoes on their way to or from a good school. This time he could look at them without envy, thinking that in a few months he would be one of them.

Crossing the road to the temple, Akash noticed the red and purple streaks reaching across the dark orange sky. As they walked on quietly Akash thought again of his last conversation with Bapu. *What you desire is on its way,* he had told him. Now Akash knew that it was true.

AUTHOR'S NOTE

India is unlike any other place in the world, and many things about this country, where I have lived for the past seven years, remain mysterious, yet endlessly fascinating, to me. In order for the reader to understand the story better I would like to give some background about Vedic math, Hindu gods, and street children in India.

As an elementary school teacher in New Delhi, I learned about Vedic math, an ancient system of Indian mathematics that was rediscovered at the beginning of the nineteenth century by an Indian mathematician. It is not taught in my school, but I found the sixteen sutras, or rules, interesting and included some of them in this book. They provide shortcuts for several mathematical operations and might even improve your mental math skills. If you would like to learn more about Vedic math you can go to this Web site: www.vedicmaths.org. It includes an introduction as well as tutorials for each of the rules.

About 80 percent of people in India practice

Hinduism, a very complex religion that includes many different gods, forms of worship, myths, stories, and rituals. For a non-Hindu the multitude of gods and their images can be confusing. While writing this book, I consulted my Indian friends and colleagues and learned that Hindu beliefs and forms of worship differ depending on geographical region or family tradition. A widespread Hindu practice is that of worshipping a particular deity to fulfill a specific material desire. For example, shopkeepers often place a statue or picture of the goddess Lakshmi in their store to ensure financial prosperity. Akash hopes for the help of Ganesha, the elephant-headed god, the remover of obstacles. Ganesha is a very popular god, often called upon by Hindus to ensure the auspicious beginning of any undertaking. Akash also worships Saraswati, the goddess of knowledge and wisdom. Her birthday is celebrated in many Indian schools and students ask for her help before exams.

One of the sad aspects of living in India is seeing the effects of poverty on children. The problem of child labor in India is closely connected to poverty. Many children have to supplement their family's income or, like Akash, work to help pay off their family's debt. Particularly in rural areas children must help their parents to work the land and tend the animals. Often the local village doesn't have a school. Or if there is a school the teacher is poorly qualified or doesn't always come to work. Officially, child labor is prohibited, but the laws are not always enforced.

Estimates about the number of street children in New Delhi range from 100,000 to 500,000. The Salaam Baalak Trust (www.salaambaalaktrust.com), one of several nongovernmental organizations working with street children, has set up a contact point at the New Delhi train station that reaches about twenty-five children a day. Many of them have run away from home, like Akash, and are vulnerable and unfamiliar with the dangers of a big city. The first goal of the Salaam Baalak Trust is to reunite the children with their parents. If this is not possible, children are encouraged to stay in one of their shelters, where they receive food, medical attention, and help continuing their education. The Salaam Baalak Trust organizes guided walking tours around the New Delhi train station and adjacent Pahar Ganj. The guides are former street children who have learned English and now expertly explain the children's plight. The tour provided me with the details for the setting of this story. Not all kids arriving without their parents at the train station receive the help of such charitable organizations. Instead they may become victims of drug peddlers who promise quick money or threaten them into their service. Some boys form groups and eke out a meager living from selling plastic bottles. Sniffing glue or whitening fluid is the cheapest way for street children to forget their pain and suffering. What I had heard and read about these kids inspired me to write this book.

A boy like Akash has only a slim chance of fulfilling his dream in contemporary India. Yet I wanted to write a hopeful book about a child who, with determination, courage, and some luck, achieves his goal against all odds.

GLOSSARY

aloo tikki: small potato cutlets

bapu: father

bhai: brother

bhangra: rhythmic dance music from the Punjab region of India

bhukki: poppy husk. When boiled and taken as a concentrate it has the effect of opium and is addictive

chai: tea

chapati: flat bread

charpoy: a bed made from a wooden frame, crisscrossed by hemp rope

coolie: a porter at the train station

dadima: grandmother (father's mother)

dal: lentils

dandia: a Gujarati dance performed with short sticks

dhabla: a shawl

dhobi: a man who washes clothes

Diwali: the Hindu festival of lights, and the most important festival in the Hindu calendar

Dussehra: the last day of Navratri, it is the Hindu festival that celebrates the defeat of the evil King Ravana at the hands of Lord Rama, the prince of Ayodhya and the seventh incarnation of Vishnu

Gandhi: Mohandas Gandhi (1869–1948), leader of the Indian nationalist movement to free India from British rule

Ganesha: the Hindu god of good luck and remover of obstacles

Ganesha Chaturthi: the Hindu festival celebrating the god Ganesha

ghee: clarified butter used in Indian cooking for frying

godhuli: dusk. The term literally refers to the dust kicked up by cows when they return from pasture

gujjar: a herder

hafta: bribe

haveli: private residence, house

Holi: the Hindu festival of colors, which is celebrated at the beginning of spring

idly: steamed cake made from rice and lentil flour; a southern Indian breakfast dish

-ji: suffix added to show respect

jird: a small, mouselike rodent with a long tail that lives in the Rajasthan desert kharif crop: the autumn harvest after the monsoon

kurta: a long shirt worn by Indian men

ladoo: an Indian sweet prepared for festivals

lathi: stick

lehnga: the traditional dress of women in northern India, consisting of a long skirt and a short blouse

lungi: a piece of cloth worn like a skirt around the waist by Indian men

mazdur: a construction worker

mela: market, fair

namaste: an Indian greeting

Navratri: the Hindu festival of dance and worship. The word literally means nine nights and refers to the nine evenings during which nine forms of female Hindu goddesses are worshipped

paan: a betel leaf filled with areca nut, lime, and spices that is chewed after meals

pahalvan: a wrestler who is sometimes used as a bouncer

puja: worship

Ramayana: the epic poem that tells the story of Rama's fight against Ravana, the ten-headed demon-king of Sri Lanka. The Ramayana is re-enacted during the festival of Dussehra and culminates in the burning of statues of Ravana

roti: a soft, flat, unleavened bread

sadhu: an Indian holy man

salwar kameez: a traditional Indian two-part dress, consisting of a long shirt over loose pants and worn with a shawl

sambar: vegetable stew with tamarind and lentils; popular in southern India

samosa: pastry filled with potatoes, peas, and cauliflower

Saraswati: the Hindu goddess of wisdom and knowledge

sari: a dress worn by Indian women, made from a long piece of fabric that is wrapped around the body and over one shoulder

Shravan: the most holy month in the Hindu calendar

Sikh: a member of the Sikh religion

teen patti: a card game

tiffin box: a box, made from stainless steel, to carry food in

tilak: a mark or dot made from herbal powder and applied to the forehead during religious worship

vahana: vehicle. The term is used to describe a god's means of transportation

Vasant Panchami: the Hindu festival that celebrates the goddess Saraswati

veena: a stringed instrument played by the goddess Saraswati

Vishnu: Hindu god, preserver of the universe

wallah: a person concerned with a particular activity, for instance, a book-wallah sells books, a chai-wallah offers tea

Yama: god of death